CUTTER
DEVIL'S CUT

j. woodburn barney

An AppalachianAcorn Book

For Deborah, as always.

For my family and friends

And especially my grandson, Weller.

Also by J. Woodburn Barney

Cutter
Cutter Director's Cut

It's easier to fool people than to convince
them that they have been fooled.

Mark Twain

ONE

MOTHER

The man tapped a cadence with his pencil to the rhythm, not of music, but of the voice of the Russian speaker he was listening in on through his oversized earphones. Every once in a while he would stop to make a quick note, then resume tapping cadence. He remained expressionless. He had the boyish good looks and easy charm which made women who met him immediately think of the bedroom. Black hair, short cropped, dark brown eyes and perfectly matched features. He was dressed in highly starched jungle fatigues, but wore no name badge, insignia or indication of rank. As a matter of record, he was a captain in a branch of the U.S. Army, a branch which had no name, only the designation of PFR. No one knew what PFR stood for, not even the nameless officers who ran it.

PFR was one of dozens of intelligence agencies that had arisen during the Cold War and, like all the others, it was fighting to remain relevant in the days after the Berlin Wall had been torn down, *détente* achieved and the Soviet Union busted up into countless numbers of uncountries. Thus far, PFR survived largely because of the political clout of the colonel who ran it. The colonel fervently believed the whole *détente* and dissolution of the Soviet empire thing was just a clever ploy by the Russians to achieve global domination. The only way to insure that didn't happen was to monitor the Russians' every move, every conversation. So the unidentified captain was a part of a team which did just that: listen to conversations.

The captain had been at this post for nearly six months, all because of his fluent Russian. It was one of five languages he had learned, with the belief the knowledge of Russian, Mandarin, Spanish, Arabic and Kinyarwanda would be helpful in getting assigned to field work in any hotspot in the world. Instead, it got him this mind numbing assignment in a gray office in a gray building amid dozens of gray buildings in a gray suburb of Prague, which thankfully was decidedly not gray. He sat, day in and day out, listening to Russian low level diplomats, left in the wake of the Soviet departure, prattle on about nothing. The assignment was made worse by his constant companion, a nameless sergeant also dressed in fatigues who stood just inside the steel door of the listening post with his hand always on the butt of the .45 automatic strapped to his hip. The sergeant and the captain never spoke, never acknowledged the other's presence. Nor did the captain and the two plainclothes guards outside the door speak.

This sergeant was the fourth guard assigned to the captain. His first guard was a huge African American corporal whose shoulders were connected directly to his ear lobes and a 48-inch chest which tapered to a 34-inch waist. The captain tried to chat the man up when he first arrived at the post, but the corporal limited his response to an expressionless "Yessir", "No, sir", or "I don't know, sir." After a few weeks of trying to befriend the guy, the captain gave up and quit talking. After two months, as he was leaving for the day, the corporal told the captain he was being reassigned and his replacement would start the next morning. The captain took advantage of the corporal's unusual loquaciousness to ask a question about something which had bothered him from day one.

"Tell me something, would you? The guards outside, they're armed with Colt M4s and grenades, enough firepower to hold off the entire village. But if the irate villagers get by them, all you have is that .45 pistol. What good do you think that would do?"

For the first time, the corporal smiled. "Sir, my weapon isn't for the villagers." He saluted, turned on his heel and marched out the door. It took a good five minutes for the captain to understand what the corporal had just told him.

Over the next few weeks, the captain thought frequently of that short conversation, and every time he thought about it, it pissed him off more. Somehow, having a personal body guard whose job it was to kill you before you could be captured by some unidentified enemy sat wrong with him. It just didn't seem sporting. Also, he would be damned if he would die over conversations about vodka and hairy Russian women. He decided he would take action, at least give himself a fighting chance. It took him a few weeks, but he finally was able to find a guy who knew a guy who had a cousin in Prague who might be able to find him a pistol of his own. The cousin did just that. The captain now had a Czech CZ75 taped under the right hand side of his desk. It was the first thing he checked every morning.

As the captain bounced his pencil, listening to a finance minister share a graphic description of the large breasts he had fondled the night before, a small red light on his desk started flashing. It meant the Russian cultural *attaché* was on his phone with Mother Russia. Since everyone in the western hemisphere knew the cultural *attaché* was in fact the head KGB agent in Prague, his communications took priority. The captain was slightly put out; he had hoped for descriptions of other portions of the minister's date's anatomy. Nonetheless, he hit the switch to catch up on what, if anything, the local KGB might be doing. Normally, the KGB report was about how the local Czech authorities were screwing up the fine system the Soviets had left in place. This time it wasn't.

This time the Kremlin was giving its local agent authority to carry out a series of assassinations aimed at disrupting the next election. The Kremlin was providing a list of who was to be eliminated and instructions on how it was to be done. The captain snapped to attention, furiously writing down every detail. Finally, finally. This was what he was here for, what PFR was here for. Maybe this assignment did matter. He had been listening to the conversation for at least ten minutes, had turned up the volume to make sure he was getting every word when the sergeant tapped him on the shoulder.

"What?" the captain mouthed.

The sergeant mimed for him to lift his earpiece. The captain did so. The sergeant pointed at the door and put a finger to his lips. The captain listened and heard faint noises from outside, then loud yelling. Finally, there was a burst of automatic gunfire. The sergeant ran toward the door and yelled into his radio, "You guys all right?" No answer. He tried again. Still no answer. They both waited

4

breathlessly. Then something hit the door, hard enough the door banged around in its frame, but did not give. They both realized it would cave soon. The sergeant turned toward the captain and unsnapped his holster. He took a step toward the captain. When all the information settled into his brain, the captain acted quickly.

He ripped the CZ75 from its hiding place under the desk, brought it to chest level and pulled the trigger twice rapidly, aiming at the center mass like he had been trained to do. Both shots hit the sergeant in the chest and as blood erupted from the man's aorta, he looked confused, took one more step and collapsed in a heap.

The banging on the door continued. The captain hit the self-destruct button on the transceiver and the equipment blew its circuits and caught on fire. He threw the pistol next to the dead guard and lay down on the floor, face down, with his hands on top of his head. He hadn't made it this far to get shot by some nervous, trigger-happy intruder.

The door finally gave way and four men dressed in military garb barged in. They too had no markings on their uniforms to indicate who, or what, they were. The captain felt a heavy boot come down on his neck, and his hands were yanked upwards violently. A plastic tie was tightened around his wrists, he was lifted to his feet and a bag was put over his head. The military men marched him out the door.

TWO

CUTTER

When I was younger and much more naive, though age has progressed more rapidly than sophistication, an English professor at Northwestern shared what he believed to be an absolute. He told us, "There are only three ways you can learn about another person: what he says, what he does and what others say about him."

"What he does" appears to be valid. The other two. Unadulterated bullshit. Take for instance, the claptrap J. Woodburn Barney has written about me. Christ in a hand basket. I tell the old guy a few stories. Actually, a lot of really good stories, and he manages to muck them up by trying to make them have some greater meaning. Like he was trying to make readers think the stories were really about his life, which, incidentally, is probably pretty meaningless. I've written a couple of short stories which were published, and yeah, I know, it wasn't like they were in *The New Yorker* or *The Atlantic*, but *Outdoor Life* is right up there with those literary bastions of our time. Ergo, I think it's time I take over telling my story. Besides, this is the good part. Note to self: Keep his editor. She does a great job. And she is very easy on the eye.

Back to the validity of what a person says or others say about him. Case in point. There are dozens of stories about how I went from being christened Winston Weller Williams to being called

Cutter. Most of them (but not all), I made up. Why? Partly because I have no idea how I got the nickname. Some because it amused folks. Mostly because I liked to create different personas for different people. Sort of creating a role for myself to fit the play I was in. Much easier than trying to justify who I may really be. Certainly more entertaining. But that is not always why others create those roles they play. Sometimes it is to escape. Or hide. Or win. Or sometimes, something worse. Way worse.

I'd driven straight through from Columbus, Colorado to Davenport, Iowa. All fourteen tortuous hours. I discovered two things: one, I was really stupid, trying to recapture my youth by buying another Wrangler; and two, after you get to Denver, watching the scenery to Davenport is like listening to twelve hours of a one note symphony. My ass was numb, my mind was numb and, because of the shit which happened in Columbus, my heart was numb. I'm not real sure why I decided to return to Davenport, but I put it down to seeing the family and returning to "Go" for a reboot. I'd called my sister Patti who was, as always, willing to put me up for a couple of days.

Patti is my go-to sibling. She's one of the older of the eight of us, I'm one of the younger. She was always good for a meal and, as long as I didn't stay more than a couple of days, she was good for a bed. And she never asked too many questions. She is the only one in the family who knew about my marital challenges and she sympathized without judgment or unsolicited advice. At any rate, I got to her place and basically slept and ate for two days. On the morning of the third day, I took her to breakfast at Ross'

Restaurant so I could have the *Magic Mountain*, Ross' infamous garbage pail meal. Think starch on steroids. Every cardiologist's wet dream.

"Well, little brother, what brings you back to the QC?"

"I dunno. I guess it's the old Fezzik logic," I told her. She smiled at the reference to the book which was required reading in our home, *The Princess Bride*. "Go back to the beginning."

"I can't imagine there is anything left here for you. Certainly you're not thinking about moving back here, are you?" It came out more as a suggestion than an inquiry. "Not many jobs around here, leastwise that you could do," she smiled.

"Yeah, I know, but I gotta start somewhere and I sure as hell don't want to go back to Des Moines." My wife, Sandy, she of the much strained marital bliss, had been a hot shot political/policy consultant there. Well, we were actually in business together, but Sandy was the one who carried the weight. I was widely regarded in those circles as her doofus husband. I wasn't sure where the marriage was headed, but I could pretty much guarantee it wasn't headed to Des Moines. Our daughter Jordan might have liked going back to be around old friends, but our son Livingston had never lived there, so I decided I could take the kids out of the equation. And I wanted the kids settled where I was so there was less chance of Sandy taking them away when and if our union finally erupted into civil war.

"So are you gonna look for a job, or just sponge off family?" We shared a family trait of subtlety.

"Maybe a tide-me-over job 'til I can figure out what I should do. The folks back in Columbus offered to give me good references if I

8

want to go back into parks work somewhere, but I may have worn out my welcome in that profession," I said. Truthfully, I had had enough of lying, cheating, conniving politicians to last a lifetime. We finished our breakfast in silence. The biscuits and gravy and greasy potatoes had begun to congeal in my stomach and I wasn't sure I could get out of the chair. The physical feeling matched my mood.

"Hey, Win, you remember my friend Barb? Barb Belville?"

"The sewing club lady?" I smirked and Patti read it perfectly. Patti and her friends had a sewing club which met once a month to drink as much wine as they could in a single evening. Hell, Patti didn't even own a sewing machine. She did own a very nice set of wine glasses.

"Yeah. The sewing club lady. Anyway, Barb said her company is looking for someone to write proposals for them. You want I should give her a call?"

"Sure," I said. What the hell, I would soon be out of money and needed to do something, anything. Patti let me pick up the check.

I touched up my *resumé* and dropped it off at Barb's office, which turned out to be right across the street from Mac's downtown. Mac's, where I spent more than a few hours with my boss when I worked for the mayor of Davenport, half a lifetime ago. Seeing how it was eleven already, I figured I'd stop in and have one of Buddy's black and tans. Never did it occur to me Buddy might no longer be there. Legend had it Buddy stood on the site and they built the bar around him. Buddy was not there.

"What'll it be? You want a lunch menu?" the young man behind the bar asked.

9

"Where's Buddy?"

"Retired. Old fuck just up and quit about two years ago. Moved to Las Vegas. Said he'd had enough. Left the place to my brother and me to run. 'Cept we don't get to keep the profits, like he did. We have to send him a third. Prick of a father, eh?"

I was kind of amazed. Buddy had owned the place? Son of a bitch. You can never tell. I offered my hand across the bar and told him, "Hi. I'm Cutter Williams. I used to spend a lot of time in here, seven, eight years ago." He shook my hand.

"Spike. Pleased to meet cha. What can I get you?"

"Can you make a black and tan?"

Spike grinned and said, "Yup. One of the few skills the old man taught me. Want some lunch?"

"No. The beer'll be enough. Thanks." Spike walked down the bar toward the taps and my phone beeped. It was a message from Barb.

"Mr. Payton asked if you could come in early this afternoon. Please call me soonest. Thanks. Barb." I called her and told her I was across the street and could be there right after I finished my lunch. I failed to mention my lunch was a beer.

She called back two minutes later to say Mr. Payton was on his way over to Mac's and would meet me there. Busted. I figured if the beer didn't play well, I probably wouldn't get along with the guy anyway. The door opened, spilling light the length of the shiny wood bar. The guy who entered got two steps into the room when Spike yelled out to him, "Hey, Marc, the usual?"

"Yessir. That would be grand."

Marc walked directly over to me, stuck his hand out and said, "Mr. Williams? I'm Marc Payton. Nice to meet you. Do you mind?" he asked, nodding to the bar stool next to me.

"Please," I told him. He looked at my beer and smiled. Either one or both of us passed the first test, and when the bartender set a generous pour of Crown Royal in front of him, I decided we both had passed.

Marc Payton was the blackest person I had ever met in my life. He was good looking with clear, very dark eyes, but I saw no clue to his age. I hate to admit this, but while African Americans don't all look the same to me, for the life of me I can never tell a black person's age. When I was in my early twenties, I was doing some human resources work for the local diocese where I caught an assignment to work with the assistant principal at one of the church's elementary schools. This principal was also African American and the most stunning woman I had been that close to. She looked to be about my age, maybe a year or two older. Certainly within my range of interest, so I turned on the old Cutter charm and pursued her. When the time was right, I asked her out. She smiled and politely declined, telling me she thought our age difference might be a problem.

"Hey, Margot, I'm very mature for my age," and I flashed my best aw-shucks grin.

"Cutter, I'm 52. Probably as old as your mother. You're cute. But not that cute." I do remember being so embarrassed my ears burned. But lesson learned. Never assume an age. So I didn't with Marc, who could have been thirty or sixty. He did own the

11

company, but that meant nothing. Not in companies which dealt in software. Those were more likely to be run by twelve year olds than sixty year olds.

Marc spent no time asking me questions. We chatted and finished our drinks, then moved to a table and ordered lunch. Thank God Mac's still had edible pizza. He told me about the company. Later, after I had passed muster with his partners and he offered me the job (at 25% more than I asked for), he explained he never asked applicants questions, but hired on the basis of the questions they asked him. It was the first clue I had to how smart Marc Payton was. Which was very.

Marc's company, which he controlled with 55% of the stock, was officially Adapted Manpower Assets Services Systems, Inc. though everyone just referred to it by its acronym, AMASS. Over the course of my series of interviews and my fleeting research on the internet, I was able to piece together the genesis and history of AMASS. About twenty years ago, Marc was working as a consultant on a project at the Rock Island Arsenal where he met Norman Pidgeon, a government employee who wrote code in the bowels of one of the hundreds of stone and brick buildings at the Arsenal. If Marc was smart, then Norman was brilliant. It didn't take Marc long to figure out Norman might be just the guy to help him turn his automated manpower tracking idea into a saleable product.

As Marc was quick to point out, the government's most valuable asset was its employees. Not valuable because those employees provided the most services, but because they cost the most. Since most bureaucrats were by inclination anal retentive control freaks, keeping track of assets was their highest priority. And any tool which would actually do that work for them would be in high demand. Marc had figured right. What he did, or more correctly, had Norman do, was design a system to track every employee in a unit, regardless of size, by assignment, job, classification, pay grade, supervisor, seniority, personal data and habits, family, friends and associates. But the true secret sauce of Marc Payton's program was he correctly foresaw the day when those employees could be physically tracked by chips on their ID cards. Or on their badges. Or in their uniforms. Or under their skin.

The ability to know instantaneously where 4.5 million employees were every minute of every day. It was enough to make even the most jaded government manager wet his or her pants. Even if AMASS only charged $100 per employee, that was a potential $450 million dollars. And Marc believed they could charge even more, especially to the Department of Defense, which never asked what a new toy cost, only what it did. And the program, once it was written and protected, cost nothing to run per employee. The annual service fee would just be the free cherry on top of the money sundae. Damn near a license to steal.

Other than his ability to prophesize manpower tracking, Marc's primary asset to the success of his company had been his ability to get potential clients to believe in him. If they believed in him, how could they not believe in what he was selling? Admittedly, he relied on his color to get his foot in the door. I quickly learned more than a few, in fact it seemed most, of the gatekeepers in federal government purchasing were African American. They had managed to form sort of an unofficial alliance which tried, with some success, to counter balance the historic advantage white owned firms had in competing for federal contracts. Not entirely counter balance, but it was a damned fine start, especially over the last several years with a black president in the White House. At any rate, over the first 15 years AMASS was in business, Marc signed them a few new clients every year, enabling them to keep afloat until the tracking chip became a reality.

Then about eighteen months ago, Marc changed. According to his partners, while he was still brilliant and still driven, he seemed to lose his ability to make the personal connections which were the backbone of sales. They not only were not getting new clients, they had started losing some they had already signed. The bleeding had continued until his partners demanded Marc bring in someone to help write proposals and do business development. That's where I came in. And why I had to pass muster with the partners who controlled the other 45% of AMASS.

Those partners included Norman Pidgeon, of course, along with Lowry Raleigh, who actually had training in manpower needs assessment and manpower planning, and Cory Jones, the youngest partner, who divided his time between running the finances of AMASS and being in charge of client entertainment. If there was a bar, restaurant or house of pleasure which a potential client might wish to visit, Cory was their guy. I liked him immediately. He was close to my age and actually still remembered how to smile, unlike the other three.

14

When Marc approached Norman about writing the computer program for his idea, Norman was hesitant. His primary worry was he would have to quit his government job which didn't bother him too much, but his wife, whom the partners referred to as "Battleax", for good reason, was disinclined to support his decision to leave. In that she was a head taller and outweighed Norman by fifty pounds, he was always deferential to her opinion. She had been known to sit on his chest to get his agreement on issues. Marc had had to give her a written guarantee he would personally pay Norman two years' worth of salary should the company go bust. Marc had no such cash reserves, so the guarantee was pretty much worthless. Not that Marc concerned himself with such trivial matters. He knew if his idea wasn't any good, he would still find a way to be lucky.

Norman's other concern was Marc's utter lack of argot. Marc couldn't speak the manpower jargon which would be all any of his potential clients would speak. So they went looking for a third partner. In the bowels of yet another building at the Rock, they found Lowry Raleigh, army manpower specialist. And boy, could Lowry speak the manpower jargon. Which turned out to be about the only language he could speak. It took Marc and Norman several multi-hour sessions over several weeks to make Lowry understand what they needed. When the concept finally settled in his brain, Lowry was all in. Besides, as an African American, he was infatuated with the idea of working for a company which would be black owned. He joined up.

The three of them set up AMASS, signed the papers and went looking for clients. It took them almost a year of living on short term loans from the bank, but they finally landed a client, a small agency in the U.S. Army known as BFDD (Bureau For Delayed Deployment). No one from AMASS had any idea what BFDD did, but it hardly mattered. BFDD had 420 employees and they wanted to track them. More precisely, the 350 pound chief personnel clerk, a black woman named Miss Gwyneth Mae, took a shine to Marc and threw her weight (figurative, not literal) around and convinced her boss to buy the program. With the stipulation Marc would spend two days a month in her office "consulting".

Marc was sitting on a bar stool in the Cubby Bear across from Wrigley Field when Norman called to tell him they had just received their first check from BFDD and wanted to know what to do with it. It wasn't until that moment they realized they needed someone to handle finances. Marc told Norman to hold onto the check and he'd get back to him.

"Can I get you another beer?" the young man behind the bar asked Marc.

"Sure. Thanks."

"What are you drinking?"

Marc realized the kid was not the same bartender who had been there when he sat down. "An Old Style, please." The kid smiled and walked over to the taps, picked up a frosted glass, twirled it in his fingers and expertly drew the beer, leaving only a few bubbles of foam running down the side.

"You look distracted," the kid said. "Everything okay?"

"Fine. Just that I was hoping to spend the day drinking beer and watching the Cubs on your giant television and now I have to go looking for someone to handle my company's finances. Pity. It's such a nice day for beer and baseball."

"Then maybe I can help," the kid said.

Marc raised his eyebrows. The kid stuck out his hand and continued, "Cory Jones. Recent University of Chicago grad in Economics, entrepreneur and bartender, *par excellence*. Looking for work. Will work for peanuts. Or a piece of the action."

Marc liked the kid's brashness. "Okay. Let's talk about the 'for a piece of the action' idea. When's good for you?"

"How about right now?"

"Don't you have to finish your shift or something?" Marc asked him.

"Oh, I don't work here. I was just showing my buddy," Cory pointed to another guy behind the bar, "how to get bartending experience without actually getting a bartending job. Just for the tips."

Marc was confused. "You don't work here?"

"Nah," Cory told him. "Place like this, big and busy, you just wait for a lull and walk behind the bar, pull a beer or two or pour a drink and everyone just assumes you belong there. Hell, I've even had managers tell me what a great job I was doing."

"And your buddy?"

"The Rickster? We do this together sometimes. Lots of fun. In exchange for me getting him behind the bar, he picks up the girls for us." Marc could see how that would work. The Rickster was a good six inches taller than Cory and had the build and looks to be a Chippendale. Seemed like a fair trade to Marc.

"So if I hire you, does Rickster come as part of the package?"

"He's a separate deal. One you probably wouldn't be interested in. As you can see, Rick has the brawn. Brains, not so much," Cory grinned.

Marc offered Cory a partnership on the spot to handle the finances and later operations. To date he had not regretted it.

As I said, I passed muster with these guys (though Lowry actually never said a word) and Marc offered me a job. But in D.C., not Iowa. They were setting up an office there to do the business development. Cory would run the office. I would be the employee. With maybe a clerk or two. Which worked even better for me. Now I had to decide how I was going to deal with Sandy. Christ in a hand basket.

THREE

CUTTER

I know. You just read that last chapter and you thought, "If he wasn't there, how could he possibly know the exact conversation between Marc and Cory?" I'll let you in on a little writers' secret. We make a lot of shit up. Don't get me wrong. Everything I'm telling you, and everything I'm going to tell you, is the God's honest truth. More or less. Over beers one night, Cory told me how he met Marc. I thought it was a pretty good story so I just added a few invented direct quotes to give it a little more pizzazz. And I'll do that again as I go along, but that doesn't mean you can't trust the story. I figure you need to be entertained as well.

Sandy. Sandra Elizabeth Surface (Morton) Williams. My wife. The smartest woman, no, the smartest person I ever met. Great looking. Terrific partner, in bed and out. Mother of the Year. Every year. Hell on wheels when she is crossed. Mary fucking Poppins. Except for one little bitty thing. She seems to have this thing about men she perceives as more powerful than she. The only way she is able to bring them down to her level, it appears, is to attack them at their weakest point: their genitals. I wish I meant she kicked them in the balls. I could live with that. Oh, no, she has to prove her superiority by bedding them, by getting them to succumb to her many charms. In all fairness, while I didn't see it in the years I knew her before we were married, it was because I ignored it. Or, more likely, I was just oblivious.

That said, she is the mother of my two favorite people in the world. Jordan, her daughter whom I adopted, and Livingston, our son. Jordan was, geez, nine at the time—going on fifteen, and Livingston was two and a half. Both of them are smart, like their mom. Only Jordan seems to be a wise ass, like her adopted dad, so it must be learned behavior. Score one for my side. Both had learned to ski, but that wasn't going to be a useful skill in D.C.. Jordan still had her horse obsession which would prove very expensive on the east coast. Sandy claimed Livingston was going to be a baseball player someday since he was, as she put it, "out in left field most of the time." He is a nice kid, but quirky.

I drove to Alexandria and met Cory at our freshly rented office on the corner of Franklin and Washington. Perfectly revolutionary. We spent a day deciding what equipment we needed and Cory gave me a set of keys to the apartment they had rented for me, not far away near the Braddock Road Metro station. I have to admit I was pretty pleased with the accommodations. Three bedrooms, two and half baths, large kitchen and very nicely furnished. I didn't find out until later that, in fact, it was damned extravagant for the D.C. area. Marc apparently wanted me to be happy. My next chore might have more bearing on happiness than his choice of accommodations. It was time I had to call Sandy. I used the apartment land line.

"Hello?"

"Hi. It's me."

"Where are you calling from?" An edge to her voice. No "It's nice to hear from you" or "I missed you." In fact, no greeting at all. Time to fish or cut bait.

20

"Alexandria, Virginia."

"What are you doing there?"

"You'll see when you come visit."

"Cutter, I just don't know. I'm not sure I can take any more of your silent treatment. I've tried to apologize. I've tried to make amends. I fucked up. I can't go back and undo the past. You get in your car and you drive away and we hear nothing for two weeks. Now you expect me to just pick up and leave and come to Alexandria?"

This was one of those very rare occasions where I couldn't find anything to say.

"Well?" Sandy's tone was getting sharper.

For what seemed an eternity all I could hear was the two of us breathing. Finally, I found my voice, "Fly into Reagan National and I promise you'll get no more silent treatment. In fact, I think we are long overdue for a conversation. Worse thing that happens: you get a really nice blue crab dinner and a mini vacation in the capital. Okay?"

It was her turn to be silent. I added, "Would it help if I said please?"

"It would."

Christ in a hand basket. "Sandy, would you please come see me in Alexandria? My treat." I fucking hate the taste of humble pie.

"Yes. Is Thursday soon enough?"

"Yep. Let me know your flight info and I'll pick you up at the airport. The kids around?"

"Yeah. I'll put them on. See you Thursday."

I chatted with the kids for a long while, got caught up on all the news and told them I would see them soon. I was shocked how much I ached when I hung up after talking to them.

The next day Cory and I started interviewing candidates for our office support positions. Actually, we interviewed only one. KC. Hired her halfway through the interview. KC Miller. KC stood for Karen Colleen, though no one ever called her that, leastwise to her face. Five foot nine, all legs, butch haircut and moved quicker than anyone I had ever met. Perky didn't even begin to describe her. Her *resumé* showed she had all the necessary skills, and when she told us about her high school basketball nickname, The Fulton Flash, we stopped the interview, hired her and dismissed the other candidates. Though probably the deciding factors were her master's degree in business from Georgetown and her two years of experience in government contracting. We offered her the total budget we had for two staff positions, hoping she could do all the work.

Over the next three days, The Flash and Cory schooled me in federal government contracting. We spent ten hours a day on the short course and by the end of it, I was pretty convinced the only thing I could bring to the table was the writing. And pretty convinced the writing was secondary, if not tertiary. The real purchasing decisions were made through wining and dining and cajoling and sweet talking and flirting and promising and threatening and scaring and any other emotion which might be utilized. All I would be doing was writing proposals so they couldn't be rejected on technicalities. Especially when the contracting agent was overcome by buyer's remorse. The work promised to be boring, but where I was and the people I was working with promised to be if not fun, at least entertaining.

Sandy arrived late on Thursday at Reagan and I picked her up and drove back to the apartment. We ordered pizza and opened a bottle of wine. As a peace offering, I let her have mushrooms and white wine. She didn't seem to notice. We talked for a couple of hours and managed to avoid any real subjects. Like her dalliance and my all-consuming anger. Instead we talked about the kids and her work. She was doing three consulting jobs from home, all for Iowa-based organizations. The most important one was with the U.S. representative from Iowa's fourth district. Congresswoman Michele Buday had recently been appointed to a subcommittee on military intelligence and needed Sandy to help tie up an education initiative she had been focusing on. You ask me, education is much more important than military intelligence (frequently the butt of an oxymoron joke) but not nearly as sexy to an elected official. Just one of the many problems plaguing Congress.

"So tell me about this job of yours," Sandy asked.

I explained what AMASS did and about my job and what I would be doing.

"Sounds frightfully tedious," she said, "but the money is pretty good."

"Yeah," I told her, "the fact the government doesn't seem to have a clue about the value of money appears to have infected government contractors as well. And AMASS is paying for this apartment," and told her what it cost.

"Holy shit, that's almost double what our house payment is! How do people afford to live here?"

"They all work for the government…" I told her. Sandy laughed. It was the first time I had made her laugh in ages.

When we had finished the pizza and wine and the update on the kids, Sandy rose, said "Good night" and went to one of the guest bedrooms. And shut the door. For some reason, it pissed me off and I pouted until I fell asleep on the couch.

I woke to the smell of coffee and bacon. I didn't remember even buying bacon, but I wasn't going to look a gift pig in the mouth. I padded to my bathroom, relieved myself, brushed my teeth and made sure my face was on straight. I wasn't used to having someone around in the morning. After my midnight pout, I decided maybe I should make a little effort. I walked into the kitchen where Sandy was set up to make our breakfast.

"Good morning."

"Good morning to you, Mr. Williams. Coffee?" Wow, this was a pleasant surprise.

"Sure. Thanks." I hesitated. "Good day, is it?"

Sandy smiled. "I hope so. What's on the agenda today?"

"I have to work half a day," I told her, "but why don't we do a little explore of Alexandria this afternoon?"

"That would be perfect." She smiled again. Christ in a hand basket, what the fuck was going on with her. "I'll go downtown and drop in to Congresswoman Buday's office. I told her I would be in the area and she asked if I had the time, could I stop by and meet her staff. And her, if she's around. How's the best way to get there?"

I took her hand (which felt very strange—I could not remember the last time we touched) and led her to the window. "Go right down there," I said, pointing at the Metro station, "and catch the Blue Line to Metro Center. That'll put you three blocks away from the House office building." She made a note of it. "Then why don't we meet back here around two and take a walking tour. I'll show you my office and we can grab an early dinner downtown?"

This time when she smiled, I decided she must be playing some kind of mind game with me. "Sounds like a plan to me," she replied and put a dish with scrambled eggs, bacon and toast in front of me. "See you this afternoon," she said, and disappeared into her bedroom.

I got back to the apartment a little before two and Sandy was already there. I changed and we walked back to my office, I introduced her to Cory and The Flash and then we spent a couple of hours admiring the buildings in Old Town. Toward the end of our walk, she sat down on the brick steps leading to a very old, very quaint brick house. "Cutter, sit," she instructed, and patted the seat beside her. I sat. "I want you to be honest with me. Do you think you can get by this? Can we make a life together?" She took her glove off and put her hand up the inside of my coat sleeve and held my arm tightly.

For the first time in eighteen months I felt affection for her. It just felt good being this close to her. "Sandy, I can't tell you how much I've missed you. Sometimes so much I thought I would go crazy. But you need to understand my faith in you has been so shaken I'm not sure how I get it back."

She smiled again. The smile could get annoying. "I'm willing to spend every day earning your trust back. Every day," and her voice trailed away as she buried her head into the shoulder of my pea coat. My eyes stung. I put my arm around her and pulled her close. We sat that way, not saying a word for ten minutes. Finally, I released her and stood up, offering her a hand.

"C'mon. Why don't I buy you a drink and some dinner?"

She continued to sit on the step, holding my hand. No smile now and for a fleeting moment I wanted it back. In a very solemn tone she said, "That's what the sailor said to the lady." I couldn't help myself. I laughed loud enough to turn the heads of passersby.

We walked up to King Street and went into the Anchor Bar at The Fish Market. The waiter was on top of us at once. "Hi, folks. Are you here for drinks or will you be joining us for dinner?"

"Both, I believe," I told him and he immediately shoved menus into our hands.

"And what may I get you to drink?"

Before I could answer, Sandy spoke up, "Two airplane gin and tonics."

"Pardon?"

She explained what an airplane gin and tonic was and he grinned and told us he would be right back with our drinks and answer any questions we had about the menu. I was grinning as well. He returned with our drinks and took our orders. I got the Jumbo Lump Crab Cakes and Sandy ordered the Crab Norfolk, which looked to me to be exactly what I had ordered, *sans* bread crumbs. But with the fancier name, it cost more. We touched glasses in a toast and I said, "To Jordan and Livingston."

She took a sip of the drink, set it on the table and got up. She walked around to my side and bent down and kissed me, not hard, but for a long time. I sort of remember our eating dinner and each drinking a large schooner of beer and I'm sure we talked, but for the life of me I don't really remember the rest of the dinner. I remember it had gotten colder by the time we left the restaurant so we gave up walking home and grabbed a cab. And made out in the back seat of the taxi.

We got back to the apartment and the scene devolved into one of those this-ain't-reality movie scenes. We started tearing at each other's clothes before we got in the door and by the time we were halfway to the bedroom, we were both naked. I'm not sure who had whom, but we both got had, right on the living room floor. And pretty much set a land speed record. Afterwards, we lay on the despoiled carpet and panted and held each other. Eventually we moved to my bedroom and followed up the animal sex with lovemaking. Much slower and much gentler. Sandy was just as receptive, if not more so. Then it hit. Suddenly my head was filled with images of her and her last, uh, indiscretion. Not that I had ever watched them, you understand. It was pure fornication imagination, but it was enough to shroud my gut with cold. I probably should have just stopped and maybe even talked to her about it. But I didn't.

FOUR

MOTHER

The captain woke in an eight by eight cell with a concrete floor and ceiling and concrete block walls, all unpainted. There was no window, a thick metal door with a slot at the bottom, a metal cot with a thin mattress, a metal commode and a single bulb on the ceiling protected by wire mesh. His head was throbbing and his eyes burned, but when he checked the rest of his body, he could find no other injuries. He was dressed in black pajamas, poorly made. He remembered being dragged out of his bunker after the unfortunate demise of his bodyguard. He couldn't help it but he smiled at the memory. He'd been unceremoniously tossed into the back of a vehicle, which started moving before he finished bouncing on the metal floor. Someone had grabbed him by the bag over his head and shoved something over his nose and mouth. One breath later he was asleep.

Over the next six or ten days, he couldn't be sure, a tray with food was pushed through the slot in the door on no apparent schedule. He tried yelling at his captors, but the sound just bounced around the echo chamber room he was in without any response. He was intrigued by the food. He would have assumed the food he would get, if any, would be MRE-like or gruel. Instead, it appeared to be lunches like a wife would pack for a construction worker husband. Heavy on the breads and cheeses, light on anything green. Had they given him a beer or two, he would have been quite satisfied.

He knew he was being softened up for whatever they had in mind for him. An environment which was the same, hour in and hour out. No change in the lighting, no change in the temperature, no sounds other than those he made, nothing to do, nothing even to look at. But he had been trained as an intelligence officer. He was prepared for this. He found ways to occupy his mind, including inventing and re-inventing the havoc he was going to visit upon his captors when the tables were turned.

On day eight or eleven or fifteen, he still didn't know, the door opened and two large gentlemen dressed in all brown walked in. The captain showed no reaction, not that it would have bothered his visitors. They each took an arm and marched the captain down a dimly lit corridor to another cell which was identical to the one he had just left, except this one had a metal desk and two chairs and no cot. He was forced down into the chair facing the desk and told to wait. His escorts left. This cell was much warmer than the one he had been in and he became aware of the stench coming off his body and clothes.

Half an hour later, a short, thin man stomped into the cell. The man was dressed in an all-black uniform with no markings except for twin lightning bolt insignias on each collar tab. He had sparse hair which was plastered down in a comb over and rimless glasses perched on a pasty face. The captain had to stifle a laugh. His captor looked like a character out of a bad Nazi movie from the early forties.

"Name."

The captain remained silent.

"Name!" This time his captor yelled. His voice was so high pitched the captain again had to stifle a laugh. The inquisitor glared at him.

Finally, the captain found his voice and answered. "Tech Sergeant Theodore Rundio. Serial number 614634332. Technical Services Support Group out of Fort Leonard Wood. On assignment in Prague to repair malfunctioning computers."

The captor rose and left without another word, just as the captain expected him to. He knew his captors would check the information he had just given them. He also knew they would discover records for Sergeant Rundio that matched what he told them exactly. That Sergeant Rundio, Ted to his friends, was what he claimed to be and that Rundio's picture would match him. They would also probably learn that Rundio had recently been shipped to Prague to repair and update old computer equipment. What they wouldn't learn is that the real Ted Rundio had died in a training accident during basic training. Not unlike numerous enlistees who had no family to notify and thus became more valuable to their country by dying and giving up their identities.

The captain was marched down to see his captor immediately after eating the next day. His captor asked him what he had really been doing in Prague and the captain repeated only what he had said before. Then the captor slapped him with what felt like a steel hand in a leather glove. Every subsequent meal led to a meeting which went exactly the same, except the beatings escalated each time. Within days, the sight and smell of food made the captain nauseous and edgy. He quit eating. He would push the food he was given back out the slot in the door. When he didn't eat, no one came for him. It worked fine until he could no longer stand the hunger and he ate one piece of bread and a tiny bite of cheese, hoping they wouldn't notice. They did and he was marched off for yet another beating.

Between the beatings, the lack of food, the smell of his own body and the endless light and boredom, the captain finally admitted he had been manning a listening post for the U.S. Army and reported what he heard to his superiors, adding that he really had never heard anything of any import. He still maintained his identity was Theodore Rundio. When he finished "confessing", the would-be Nazi left the cell without a word.

The captain was not returned to his cell. This time he was led into a much larger cell, one which was nicely painted and furnished with real furniture, including a couch, a writing desk, a television, a large bed and a full bathroom. Lying on the bed were a complete set of clothes, toiletries, a stack of tapes and a newspaper. He grabbed the toiletries and immediately headed to the shower. He stood under the hot water until long after he thought it might turn cold. He couldn't bring himself to leave it. Finally, he was stirred from the utter bliss by the smell of warm food. He toweled off as quickly as he could and found a small table laden with a huge dinner, including Budweiser beer. And not the American pretender Budweiser but the original Czech brand.

After he consumed as much as he could eat, which was very little, he noticed a bottle of Crown Royal with a bucket of ice and two crystal whiskey glasses. He blinked. He couldn't believe his apparent good fortune, and quickly poured himself a glass full of liquor over ice, picked up the newspaper and the tapes and settled on the couch. He looked through the tapes and found they were all

American movies, all action, which were his favorites. He picked up the paper, stared at it, and dropped his glass of whiskey.

The captain was not surprised or shocked by the headlines. What shocked him was the name of the paper. The *Roanoke-Chowan News-Herald*. The newspaper which served his hometown of Ahoskie, North Carolina. Not the hometown of Theodore Rundio, Columbus, Ohio. But his, the captain's own hometown. How the hell had they done that? For that matter, how had they known what his drink of choice was? He tried to remember whether he had been drugged or so out of it with hunger and pain that he had somehow told them who he really was. No, he was positive he hadn't been given any drugs, and he knew he hadn't cracked from their torture. Even when he told them what he had been doing he had stayed in character.

The captain drank two glasses of whiskey and went to sleep. Never had a bed felt as good. He woke naturally, took another shower and shaved. Just as he was finishing there was a knock on the door to the cell. Since there was no peephole or doorknob, he did nothing. A full minute later the door opened a crack and a voice said, in perfect English, "I have your breakfast. May I come in?" Perhaps perfect English was not quite correct, he thought to himself. This English was actually the Lumbee English dialect, the one he had grown up with. Hearing it froze him, speechless.

The voice asked again, "May I come in? Your breakfast is getting cold."

The captain nodded, then realized his visitor could not see him and answered, "Yes. Please."

32

A black woman entered, pushing a small table with covered dishes, a carafe of coffee and a pitcher of orange juice. She smiled at the captain. She was young, with pitch black hair and perfectly smooth skin. Teeth so white they sparkled. Her looks were what in the old days would have been described as "handsome". The female equivalent of a tall, dark stranger. She quietly went about preparing his table and then invited him to sit by waving her hand at a chair. He sat. Her presence was somehow almost comforting and that thought put him on guard.

"May I have a cup of coffee and join you?" she asked.

"It's your party," was the best he could respond. She first poured a cup of coffee for the captain and then one for herself. Black for him, like he liked it, but without asking him. Lots of cream in hers. She moved slowly and with an immense grace. She settled onto his couch.

"Can we talk, Anthony? Or may I call you Tony?" she asked quietly.

The captain blew hot coffee through his nose and began choking. How the fuck did she know? How had they discovered his true identity? He wiped the coffee from his face and told her, "You talk. I'll listen." She did.

FIVE

CUTTER

Something cold and implacable had made itself at home during my connubial reunion with Sandy. It was a new sensation for me, this deadness, especially when it came to Sandy. Understand, I have a dark side, one I try to keep hidden from others. I hid it from ole J. Woodburn when I told him my earlier stories. You read the things he wrote about me and he makes me sound pretty much even keeled and positive. Even my flirt with mental illness, the period when I couldn't control my emotions and every day was another terror to endure, even that Barney glossed over.

That dark side, that blackness, seemed to welcome this new sensation of coldness. Like it made it okay for me to be a shit, particularly to Sandy. I was two-faced about it. I treated her as if I was the guy Barney made me out to be, but I know, while she couldn't put her finger on it, there was an underlying meanness to my every day dealings with her and she had to feel it. But I'd be damned if I let it, or her, separate me from the kids. Fuck love. Seems to me it gains you nothing except royal pains in the ass. And occasionally gets you laid.

I kept the job at AMASS and spent lots of hours at work and meeting potential clients for drinks and dinners. Anything to keep me out of the lonely apartment and my mind occupied. Sandy returned to Columbus, Colorado to sell the house and to put the whole Wild West chapter behind us. I don't know if she saw her ex-paramour and to my surprise, I found I really didn't care one way or the other.

Over the next several months we drifted into a new East Coast life. We bought a house in Friendly, Virginia (which turned out to be anything but), got the kids settled in school and pre-school, Sandy joined a church and we tried to establish a social life. Sandy did her consulting work at home, most of it for Congresswoman Buday. After she finished her first three projects for the Congresswoman, Mrs. Buday offered her a position on her staff. The guys at work were really pleased to hear about that, right up until Sandy warned me that in no way could she help us get contracts—it would be a breach of ethics rules. Not like everybody else didn't breach those same rules. Of course, Sandy would pick this issue to be ethical. Marriage vows, that was an entirely different matter.

In the late fall, Marc called an all-hands staff meeting. The business was doing okay. The Flash and I had booked a few new contracts and ended the federal fiscal year, which was September 30, by signing a substantial contract with the Army Corps of Engineers. In fact, the contract was large enough KC (The Flash) and I, along with Cory, had to put aside our normal hats and get involved in operations. Finally, I got an assignment I was comfortable with. After numerous consulting gigs and a few years running a parks department, if nothing else, I knew how to delegate. I handled the hiring and set up a space and the training for the new folks, about twelve of them. The Flash handled the contracts side and Cory took care of all the administration problems. Norman and Lowry's faces lit up when I announced the deal. Finally they could get back down in the weeds and not worry about the big picture of running a business. I suspected a large part of their smiles was from learning they would both be putting a big wad of money in their pockets. They both said thanks, but no one said a word about putting a wad of any size in my pocket.

At any rate, it was odd that Marc announced the big staff meeting. While everyone else had gotten pretty excited about the new business, Marc had told us a quiet "Thanks for your work," and basically retired to his office where he kept his door closed and spent hours on the phone. He acted jumpy and distracted and we all quickly caught on to leave him alone. He attended no meetings, took no calls. The morning of the meeting he showed up dressed in a new suit and looking, as KC described it, "Pretty damned fine." He was smiling and went around greeting each person in the office, joking and laughing. It was a nice change. He had KC order in a smorgasbord of sandwiches and finger food. After we were all gathered in the conference room, Marc wheeled in a caddy loaded with a dozen bottles of expensive champagne on ice and flutes which he personally passed out. We all applauded and Marc led us in a toast.

"On behalf of myself and the other owners, I want to thank each and every one of you for the outstanding work you have done over the last year. I would especially like to acknowledge the great contributions some of the newbies have made. KC, your work ethic and production levels have set a new standard for the company. Julie Barney, the changes you recommended and then made to our software have turned a very functional workhorse into a program which is so user friendly no one in their right mind would not want it in their office. And Cutter, while I can't see any real work you do," and here Marc paused for the laughter he expected and got, "you brought in the biggest contract we have ever had and you somehow managed to make us all have fun doing it."

I flashed my aw-shucks grin at the table but then rubbed my thumb and forefingers together indicating I wanted money to go with the praise. That also got a laugh and everyone started rubbing their fingers together.

Marc continued, "I want everyone to schedule time off during the holidays, though telling Cutter to schedule time off is like telling the sun to rise every morning." More laughs. Apparently it was Cutter-as-punch-line day. "Things are going to get hectic here after the new year starts. We will officially be in the silly season." He paused to make sure everyone was following. Most of the techie folks were not, though only Julie raised her hand.

"Yes?"

"I don't know what that is," Julie said.

"It's the start of the campaign season for president. It used to be it lasted about six months. Now we have to put up with a whole year's worth of bullshit. Conventional thought is after two terms with a Democrat in office the tendency would be for people to elect a Republican. But everyone loves the vice president and he is sure to throw his hat in the ring. That, added to the fact the Republicans have allowed their party to be hijacked by the reactionary fringe, means it's anyone's ballgame. I bring this up because it is absolutely paramount none of us get involved with the campaigns. We want to stay everyone's friend."

"I'm not telling you how to vote—vote your conscience. But please make no public statements, no bumper stickers, no yard signs, nothing which can come back to haunt us all. Understood?"

Lots of head nods. Just one question, again from Julie. "So who do you think we should vote for?"

Marc smiled. "The best candidate. The best of course being the one most likely to give us more contracts."

Julie persisted, "How do we know which one that will be?"

Marc's smile turned to a huge grin. "I'll tell you." More laughter. He followed with a briefing on the latest contracts and tried to make sure everyone was on the same page. He offered his partners the opportunity to say a few words. They all declined. Finally he turned to Cory and asked, "You have any idea where Brandon is? I need to talk with him."

"Sorry, Marc. Haven't any idea where he is. Just because we have the same last name doesn't make me his keeper. But if I hear from him, I'll let you know. Don't wait up for it."

"Okay." Marc frowned and surveyed the room. "Anyone else have anything?"

Once again, Julie raised her hand. "Does AMASS do a Christmas party?" Everyone except us new folks applauded and whooped and hollered. "What? Did I say something wrong?"

Cory smiled. "No, Julie, it's just we have a time-honored tradition here. The first person who brings up the Christmas party gets to be in charge of it. Congratulations! We're all excited to see what you come up with." Now everyone applauded. Except Julie, who just blushed.

The only reason I even bring up this party, which has absolutely nothing to do with the story, is because that's where I met Julie's cantankerous father, J. Woodburn Barney. I was dateless (Sandy said it would be "unethical" for her to attend a contractor's party) and J. Woodburn is pretty antisocial. We ended up next to each other at the bar. I ordered an airplane gin and tonic and he got a kick out of my description of the drink so we started chatting and I turned raconteur. He claimed to be a writer, unpublished, of course, and I told him about my literary achievements, like the short story in *Outdoor Life*. He thought he could turn some of my stories into something, so I agreed to meet him occasionally to swap lies. As long as he bought the beers. Which he did. Come to think of it, I may have to ask him to help with this story. There was a lot that had happened before I got involved and stuff we learned afterwards which didn't involve me directly. Maybe I'll get him to write those parts.

The meeting broke up and as we were leaving, Marc pointed at me and then at the chair next to him. I sat.

"Cutter, I've been thinking. With our good fortune with the Army Corps, maybe we should do a little giveaway marketing."

"I don't follow," I told him.

"Make a donation of our services to a couple of agencies in exchange for the good will, the tax write-off and, of course, their endorsement and advocacy."

"Great idea. The Flash and I will look around and see who might be interested."

Marc frowned. "You don't have to do that. I've already decided which agencies I want to give it to. All you have to do is get them to accept it."

"Sure. Who'd you have in mind?"

"FEMA, the CDC and USAID. All three agencies do work almost everyone supports and all are small enough to not break the bank."

"I'm on it, Boss."

"Cutter, I want this done before Christmas—we need the write-off this year. Since you'll have to go to Atlanta to meet with the CDC folks, I suggest you start there. Get Barb to book you a flight and start making calls to set up appointments. Get a move on." Just like that, gregarious Marc was gone and sullen Marc was back. I excused myself and began learning a little about the agencies I would be talking to.

An hour later, I knocked on Marc's door and stuck my head in. "What now?" he barked.

I entered and stood before his desk. "Marc, between the three agencies, they have almost as many employees as the Corps of Engineers, like 35,000. That means we'll have to add yet another ten to twelve folks to staff."

"Goddamnit, Cutter, why can't you just do what I ask?" he snarled and fell silent. I just stood there shifting from one foot to the other. "Fine," he said, "don't do USAID. Now get to work." I knew better than to point out USAID was by far the smallest of the agencies and would only reduce the number of employees by 4,000. I went to work.

Two weeks later I met with Ellen Thordarson, assistant to the director at FEMA. She was quite charming and welcoming and spent several hours listening to my spiel. She assured me they would take it under advisement and get back to me after the holidays. I explained our tight time frame and she promised to see what she could do. I heard nothing for two weeks, but when I called her back mid-December, she asked me to come see her staff because they were going to accept the offer. Whew.

I flew to Atlanta in early December and met with Dr. William Hoy, head of human resources for the CDC. I made my presentation, though between the numerous times his assistants interrupted us and his glazed demeanor, I am pretty sure he didn't get what I was offering. He let me finish and then told me, "I greatly appreciate your generous offer, but I think we will just stick with our current system. It suits our needs just fine."

I tried again, "But, Dr. Hoy, what we're offering has capabilities far beyond the system you are using now AND we are providing it with absolutely no cost to you. We can even arrange to keep your current system as a backup until you are completely comfortable with the new one." I could tell from his expression I was not only not getting anywhere, but that, at least with him, I never would. I flew back to D.C. empty-handed. Maybe Marc would let me switch back to USAID.

He didn't.

"Williams, you have to get this done. I don't care how, but when I want to give something away, Goddamnit, I want to give it away. Go get this done. No excuses."

Christ in a hand basket.

I shared my problem with Sandy while we were having a glass of wine that evening. I couldn't believe it but she actually offered to help. She pointed out that Hoy must have a boss and she'd have someone in Congresswoman Buday's office call to see if that person would see me. She was quick to remind me this was only because we were donating the program to the Center for Disease Control and she couldn't help open any doors for sales.

I flew back to Atlanta and five days before Christmas met with Dr. Kathleen Frye, Assistant Director for Administration, Hoy's boss. Frye, unlike Hoy, was attentive and asked pertinent questions. At the end of the presentation, she told me she and the Director really wanted to thank me for coming back down, but that our program was way beyond their needs, currently or in the foreseeable future. Thanks, but no thanks. I returned to D.C. to tell Marc.

"Cutter, this is unacceptable. You know how important this is to me. I'm not sure how you can expect to sell something you can't even give away." Marc's face darkened even more than normal. He lowered his head and rubbed his temples as if he had a headache. He did this for what seemed like a long time and then shook his shoulders and jumped up from his chair, knocking it over backwards.

"Get the fuck out of my sight. Get the fuck out of the office. Get the fuck out of my organization, you worthless piece of shit. Pack your stuff up and get the fuck out now!" By the time he got to the end he was screaming, on full rage setting. I backed out of his office, packed my stuff and went home.

My airplane gin and tonic contained no tonic. Three days until Christmas and no job. I was beginning to think I was a jinx. A Jonah. The kids were at the sitter's and Sandy was at her Christmas office party (contractors not invited, though now I could have gone, I suppose) so I was alone for the evening. For the first time ever, I was scared to death of being out of a job. Before this, I always felt in charge of my own destiny, at least work wise. Maybe not so much love-life wise. This was the first time I had been fired and frankly it sucked.

I had been home for about three ounces of gin when the doorbell rang. It was Cory, who stood at the door with a bottle of Williams Chase Gin, the good stuff, and wearing a huge grin. "Need a drink, Cowboy?" he asked.

"It's not funny. I am seriously fucked, Cory."

"No you're not. Marc sent me over to give you this bottle and to apologize for him and to beg you to come back. He was just having an off day."

"Off day, my ass. The man is crazy. Looney. Mad as Caligula. You should have seen him. I thought he was going to go postal on me."

Cory thought for a few minutes and finally said, "Get me a glass with ice and some tonic and let me explain." I did as he asked and we sat down at the dining room table.

43

"Remember when I told you how Marc changed a couple of years ago?"

"Yeah."

"He is basically suffering from PTSD. Sometimes he can't control his emotions."

"What happened to him?" I asked.

"Two and a half years ago, Marc attended a huge family reunion in Ahoskie, North Carolina where he grew up. His family has deep roots there. They've been in that area since before the Civil War. He was staying with his mother and siblings for the week. Apparently one night he went in search of a drink at the local tavern with an old friend and spent several hours reminiscing and getting drunk. About midnight, they heard a large explosion. Turned out it was his mom's house. A gas leak. Burned to the ground. Marc lost his mother, his twin brother and his baby sister. All the immediate family he had.

"Marc was inconsolable. He spent several days in the hospital sedated. When he finally returned home, he was morose, angry at everyone and everything. His wife tried but she couldn't take it. She moved out six months later. He acted like he didn't care. Frankly, Cutter, I don't think he did care. I think he cares for no one now."

"Son of a bitch," was all I could think to say.

SIX

MOTHER

"So, Anthony, we obviously know who you are and why you are in Prague. We know you have been trained in tradecraft and that you were top of your class. When we came to visit your 'office' it was our intent to steal your technology and send a message to your government. We also thought we might be able to use you as a bargaining chip. What we did not expect was for you to do what you did, murder your comrade in arms. Coldly and obviously planned in advance."

The captain smiled.

The woman continued in her high country drawl. "We have reconsidered our position. It appears we can assume two things about you. One, your devotion to self is stronger than any patriotism or code of honor or *esprit de corps* and two, you have little or no compunction about taking whatever action is necessary to advance your own objectives."

Again the captain smiled. But said nothing.

"We will make you an offer. Understand, should you elect not to accept it, we will go back to our original plan and see if you are worth anything as a bargaining chip. We, of course, cannot guarantee your government will agree to take you back, in which case you will be tried by the Czechs as a spy. Nor can we guarantee if your government does take you back that they will not try you for murder. I would think, as any reasonable person would, you would accept our offer. But you are not reasonable, so we leave the choice to you." She lapsed into silence.

The captain finally asked, "Who is the 'we' making the offer?"

Now it was the woman's chance to smile. "Why Mother Russia, of course. I'm surprised you have to ask. You know, your boss was on the right path when he claimed *détente* was all a ruse. We had to rid ourselves of all those suckling satellite countries before they bankrupted us entirely. The KGB eventually made our leaders see this."

"What's the offer?"

"You help us when we need it."

"Wet work?"

"No. In fact, we don't have anything in mind now. You just need to be available when we need you. If we need you. Failure to keep your end of the bargain would result in termination of the contract with extreme prejudice. Understand?"

"Of course I understand. You kill me. And probably anyone around me." The captain paused. Then, "What do I get out of it?"

"You mean besides your life and most of your freedom?"

"Like you said, pretty lady, I have a very high devotion to self."

"We place you in a position where you get a substantial income with little or no work, and we make annual payments to an offshore account which will come to you after your service is complete."

"All right. Now what?"

"Well, you need to lose some weight."

"What the hell do you mean? I'm in great shape." The captain was actually offended by this. Not by selling out his country, but by being accused of not being in good shape.

"We have to explain your capture and imprisonment. Your backstory is you have been kidnapped by members of Donetsk People's Republic, tortured and will be offered in exchange for a ransom."

The captain looked confused. "What does a Ukrainian terrorist group have to do with any of this?"

"Nothing except when Russia offers, in the spirit of international relations, to intercede on America's behalf, your government will not have to refuse to pay the ransom. And Russia is known to have influence over Donetsk. So we dress you to make it appear you have been beaten and mistreated, shoot some video demanding money and broadcast it on the internet. An internet site which will be traced to deep in the heart of the Ukraine. Then over the next three months, you will be schooled in our practices while you lose weight."

What she failed to point out was to make sure the abuse part of the story was verifiable, the captain was also beaten and had a couple of bones broken and teeth knocked out during the same time period, but in such a way no scars remained, at least no physical ones. By the time he was turned over to the American government he looked the part of a prisoner of war. He certainly no longer made women think of the bedroom when they saw him.

He was debriefed and his story matched up with what the Americans knew. Right down to how the sergeant guarding him had died defending the captain. The captain spent a month in an army hospital and was then allowed to resign with full honors and the thanks of his government. As far as they were concerned, he was damaged goods.

Within a few days of returning home he was contacted by an official with the Connard Corporation and offered a job. The official used the magic words the former captain had been expecting to hear. "Mother has a job for you." He noted the time and place of the meeting and two days later drove to Norfolk International Airport where a ticket waited for him to Connard International Waikiki on Saratoga Road, Honolulu. He was booked into a six room suite and he spent three days enjoying the restaurants, bars, spa and beach before he was approached by a young man who told him, "Mother has a job for you."

"Sir," the young man said, "Mother would like you to accept our offer as the assistant head of security for Connard International Resorts. You will be required to spend forty weeks a year in our resorts here and in our other thirteen properties in America, Scotland, Canada and wherever else we may build. Your duties will be to spend time at the resorts, shake some hands, play some golf and whatever else Mother may decide. Largely you will be on vacation those weeks. What you do with the other weeks of the year is up to you. Your salary will be $175,000 a year plus expenses. Do you have any questions?"

"Only one. Why Connard International? I am under the impression that Harry Connard is a flake. Will this business hold up?"

The young man smiled. "As you may remember, Mr. Connard inherited two resorts from his father and within four years had managed to bankrupt one and leave the other in dire straits. As a business man, he was a complete and total dud. All he had going for him was a supersized ego. So Mother stepped in and made him an offer. She would bankroll him and he would become an employee of Mother, just as you have."

"You mean Connard International is a Russian company?"

"Oh, no, sir. It is entirely American. Only Harry Connard is owned by Mother."

"And you?"

"I am an employee of Connard International just like you, sir. In fact, I will be working for you."

The captain took the job and spent almost twenty years traveling from Connard resort to Connard resort. Not once did he hear from Mother. He marveled that a company as poorly run as Connard International could not only keep going but also continue to grow. Harry seemed to be a golden child. His fame grew and he even managed to buy himself a reality television show through which he became a household name. The captain assumed the constant influx of capital came from Mother, but he never asked.

He was having dinner with his family when Mother next called. The call was made by his assistant. "Mother has a job for you. Meet me in Sax Grill and Lounge in fifteen minutes." The captain did as he was told.

After several hours and several drinks, his assistant told him, "I hate to tell you this, but your brother is going to meet with an unfortunate accident and Mother needs you to assume his life. From this point on Anthony will no longer exist—he is the one who will die in the accident. You will become Marc."

The captain stared at Brandon and was about to scream "No" when they heard the explosion. Brandon Jones handed Anthony all of Marc's identification papers and told him they would be in touch. Anthony Payton was now Marc Payton, CEO and owner of AMASS.

SEVEN

CUTTER

After the holidays I returned to work, though I have to admit it was with some trepidation. I decided I should keep my helmet on, my flak jacket zipped and my options open. Within ten minutes of my arrival Marc was at my desk asking me to join him in his office. I followed him in and he motioned for me to close the door.

"Cutter, I need you to assume a new role with AMASS. We have grown so quickly, largely thanks to you, Cory is unable to keep up with all his work. I need him to focus on finances and investments and not have to worry about operations. I'd like you to be our Chief Operating Officer." He smiled. Had he added, "I ate his liver with some fava beans and a nice chianti," I could have not been more surprised. From my new perspective he was the black Hannibal Lecter. "Well?" he demanded when I had said nothing.

"Sorry, Marc," I said. "I'd be honored to accept, though I think I would like to have a contract with certain assurances."

"Fine. Whatever you would like. Want to keep my valuable people happy." Again he smiled, then added, "I do want to apologize for what happened a couple of weeks ago. Occasionally it all gets to me. Cory may have told you I have a form of PTSD and it sometimes just takes over. You shouldn't worry. If I blow up at you, give me a few hours to cool off. We'll be fine."

I took off my helmet but didn't unfasten my flak jacket. I wasn't sure if it was his way of saying he was sorry, or whether he thought the new job would be that much harder, but he doubled my salary. I was elated, of course, though it made me feel a little, what, bought and paid for. Which made me feel uneasy.

KC took over all the business development duties, and I focused on getting new people in to handle the new contract with FEMA. I spent the next several months learning the intricacies of what AMASS actually did, how the software worked and how our services were delivered. Over time, it became obvious to me that while our secret sauce was indeed pretty amazing stuff, the way we delivered the services was damned near archaic. I dove into designing a more efficient operating system. Once I had it mapped out, I asked Sandy to look it over.

Sandy read my manual all the way through, then without a word, read it a second time. "Well, do you think it will work?" I finally asked.

"Cutter, I can't believe it, but you actually must have been paying attention all those years. This looks great to me." I grinned. Then she gave me the dozen or so changes she thought might improve it. I sighed. And made her changes. Some things remained the same.

I met with Marc and the other partners the next day and laid out the plan. Not unexpectedly, Norman had nothing to say, Lowry wanted to study the plan, at length, and Cory was a little miffed because I was basically jettisoning his entire way of doing business. I think he was also still pissed about the amount of money Marc was paying me, though he never said anything. Marc told me he'd get back to me. Two hours later, he gave me the all clear to proceed.

Over the next couple of months, with a lot of help from The Flash, and a surprising amount from Cory, AMASS made the switchover and almost immediately saw a fifteen percent increase in the profit margin. Cory recommended a bonus for The Flash and me. Lowry sent me an email saying he thought my plan might work and suggested we try a test run for six months. Norman still said nothing.

While we all busied ourselves trying to get rich sucking at the mother of all public teats, that mother was busying herself trying to give away all the milk in the national coffers. Marc explained to me a federal buying frenzy (and our subsequent feeding frenzy) always occurred before a new president was elected. This frenzy was particularly voracious this election in that all of the eight republican candidates were promising to cut to shreds all the budgets except the military's. Our service was particularly attractive to those nonmilitary agencies in that we promised it would save them money in the long run. The military, of course, wanted to spend because, well, they always want to spend. A ten-dollar screw, great. A five-hundred dollar hammer, terrific. A nine-thousand dollar chair, outstanding. No cost too great to keep our country safe. And our generals happy.

The election was promising to be one of the most outlandish and entertaining I had ever witnessed. Eight Republican candidates and three or four Democrats, plus the usual slew of minor party wannabes. Most surprising was normally the country would drift toward the more moderate candidates, but most of the moderate candidates, representing both sides, failed to get any traction at all and would soon be eliminated from the competition.

Before I get any further into the whole election fiasco, I think I should tell you, in all fairness, my political prejudices. I'm going to try not to let those prejudices influence this story (and I sure as hell don't think they have anything to do with the outcome), but you do have the right to know what eyes you are looking through when you read this. Although if like most folks you're tired of hearing political opinions, feel free to skip the next eight paragraphs. As my daughter Jordan told me one night when I was railing at a candidate on TV, "Dad, shut your pie hole."

J. Woodburn once pointed out to me I had won the lottery the day I was born. Large family of caring people, good community, male, white and born in the USA. That gives me a leg up on 99.99+% of the world's population. And I am grateful for that. Every problem I have ever had comes under the heading "First World Problems." We believed in the American Dream—work hard and enjoy the fruits of your labor and be free to do whatever you want. The American ideal of hard work rewarded, I had been surprised to learn, was pretty much an invention of Jonathon Edwards and Ben Franklin who were both trying to sell something to people who had very little. Edwards was selling religion and Franklin was selling newspapers. Even the American ideal was a profit driven concept.

I believe in capitalism. But not as the be-all, end-all. An economic system has to take into account man's most basic drive, greed (sadly, not sex or beer). But the system has to have controls on it if it is to survive. I've always loved Lincoln's line from *The Gettysburg Address*, "Now we are engaged in a great civil war, testing whether

54

that nation, or any nation, so conceived and so dedicated, can long endure." While he was talking about the concepts of individual freedom and democracy, he failed to take into account the two most horrifying examples of greed upon which this nation was actually built: the mass genocide of about 15,000,000 Native Americans and the enslavement of 12,000,000 Africans and their progeny. Our forefathers stole the natural resources and the labor to build a country. If the white people of America spent 500 years trying to atone for that greed, it wouldn't be enough.

So I think the federal government should represent new ideals. Government should exist to provide those services, and only those services, which are for the public good but which the free market will not support. By public good, I mean for all of a government's citizens, not just the fortunate. Republicans want the free market to take care of everything. It assumes the America that exists is the imaginary one created by Edwards and Franklin, where all that stands in the way of anyone being happy, healthy and well off is his or her willingness to work hard. That everyone here started with a share of the products of resources and labor stolen from our predecessors. Well, everyone didn't.

In the 1970s and 80s this country experienced a cataclysmic disruption to its labor force which was unlike anything we had ever experienced. During the second half of the fourteenth century the black plague killed one third of Europe's labor force. All of a sudden, land owners were begging for help to farm their lands. For the first time the labor force could demand more of a share of the wealth. It was the beginning of a middle class, an economic class which reached its zenith during the 1950s and 60s right here in the good old USA. Then came the disruption.

Overnight the labor force grew by almost one third. Suddenly women joined the workforce. This was terrific. For far too long women's abilities and efforts were unrecognized by a male centric society. But the huge growth in employed women was not matched by any reduction of men in the workforce. Almost immediately, the company owners realized they had a new cheaper source of labor. The result was the opposite of the black plague. It dealt a devastating blow to the middle class. Not only were laborers much more plentiful, but the more educated (and therefore more employable) men and women tended to marry each other and less employable men and women had to take lesser jobs. At lesser pay. Whites got richer, people of color got poorer.

Did the government take any action to counter this loss of economic balance? Hell, no. Unless you count helping destroy unions, authorizing predatory banking and insurance industry policies, trying to export a government system built on greed and allowing industry to ship jobs away from this country. Yeah, the feds did that, mostly under the guise of "trickle down" economics.

Now we're having an election which pits the haves against the have-nots. With no middle ground and with lots of pent up anger and frustration. I was looking for a candidate who would see the problems, see the long term outcome from those problems and address those issues. Not what I, or anyone else for that matter, got.

I wanted a candidate who would propose to lead us from a society of greed to a society of mutual benefit. Old man Barney said I might as well wish for wings and fairy dust. Nonetheless, I argued with the old coot that, for the public good, the government should launch a full scale attack on greed itself. How? Enact a minimum wage which at forty hours a week would support two people above the poverty level. No management employee of a publicly held company can earn more than twenty times the wage of the lowest paid employee of that company. Limit what a person can inherit to a sum equal to the national average cost of a house or two per cent of the value of the estate, whichever is higher. A 98% estate tax. Limit individual gifts to half that amount each year. All the remaining estates pass to the government to provide free health care to everyone and for upkeep of the nation's infrastructure. Let everyone reap the rewards of their own efforts, not the efforts of their ancestors. I ran this idea by a number of friends and acquaintances and their reaction was exactly like you would predict. Liberals thought it a fine but totally unrealistic plan, conservatives thought it terrible and unfair and middle of the roaders just shook their heads. The only outliers, and there were enough to make me see I was on the right track, were those liberals and middle of the roaders who had inherited money. To a person they said it would be totally unfair. One woman nodded her head violently in agreement with my spiel on greed right up to the point she realized she and her siblings would not have inherited the millions her father left them. She protested a 98% estate tax would be so unfair because, in her words, "Well it just is. That's why." J. Woodburn told me I was crazy. He's no doubt right, but I would still support the candidate who seemed to be the most anti-greed. Christ on a milk carton was I going to be sorely disappointed.

Okay, if you skipped the political diatribe, this is where you can come back in. I'm not going to rehash all the names and backgrounds of all the initial candidates because everyone already knows all that. Also-rans never have and never will merit anything more than a foot note in a history book.

We first got a glimpse of the coming attraction at the very first Republican debate. All eight hopefuls lined up in a row, each given three minutes for an opening statement. The moderator went straight down the line, each candidate spewing forth a statement, all of which, when reduced to their essence, said, "Pick me, pick me. I'm the best." Except for the eighth and final speaker.

The final speaker was the surprise wild card candidate, Harry Connard, he of resort and reality TV fame. He had absolutely no qualifications for the job, but his ego and bankroll were enough to get him a seat at the table. Everyone, including me, assumed he was just living out some kind of bucket list fantasy and would quickly become one of those also-rans. We thought that right up to his first debate.

When it was Harry's turn for an opening statement, he smiled his big toothy grin and rubbed his bald head. Then he spoke. "Folks, you all know me and what a great businessman I am. All these other people up here are politicians and, since I know each and every one of them, I can tell you what they really are." Here he paused for effect and then pointed at the candidate farthest to his right. "He's an asshole." There was an audible gasp from the audience. The moderator tried to interrupt, but Harry pressed on and pointed to the next person, who happened to be female. "Bitch." His finger moved down the line. "Jew. Faggot. Pussy. Cheat. Bigot."

The stage erupted in mayhem, everyone trying to talk at once, the moderator ineffectively trying to regain control. Four of the candidates left the stage. The remaining contestants yelled at Harry and each other. Harry shook his head and then bowed it, as if in sadness. What he was really doing was trying to hide his grin. The anchor for the broadcasting network finally cut in and talked over the melee. With the proper amount of decorum, the anchor solemnly pronounced the debate over and added he sincerely doubted if Harry Connard would be invited to participate in any future debates.

Unfortunately for the political process, the anchor was dead wrong. The internet lit up with comments and memes and the video was played 200,000,000 times. Every network, every news outlet, every on-line commentator and every blogger instantly realized they had a genuine take-it-to-the-bank hit on their hands. The more they could get Harry Connard on their screens or on their pages, the more viewers and readers they would have and, most importantly, the more money they could make. Contrary to what the anchor hoped for, presidential politics was now the entertainment hit of the year. P. T. Barnum stood up from his grave and applauded.

The Connard, as the internet started calling him, took his show on the road. He drew huge crowds and his message was the same everywhere he went. "No more political correctness. Get rid of the outsiders. I will give you back what is rightfully yours." Each of his followers interpreted what he said according to their own needs and their own fears and their own prejudices. No more "political correctness" meant you could say anything you liked, about anyone, anytime. "Outsiders" meant Muslims to the Mexicans, the Mexicans to the blacks and anyone of color to the whites. "Rightfully yours" meant anything anyone wanted. His rallies often ended in violence, violence he encouraged. The cameras and reporters followed him every step of the way. No other candidate could be heard because all eyes were focused on The Connard. Every day he did something or said something even more outrageous to insure the coverage stayed on him. The strategy was brilliant. Scary, but brilliant. He had somehow been able to switch the political paradigm from richer versus poor to rich and poor versus poorer.

In the meantime, the Democrats went quietly about their business. Since it was quite apparent Vice President James Breiner would be their choice to run, no one, certainly not the press, gave them any attention. They knew when voters got into the booth in the primaries, they would come to their senses and choose a reasonable candidate. The only question facing the Democrats was who their opponent would be in November and how they would counter the fomentation of hate rising over the country.

At AMASS we spent time joking about the idiocy of the campaign to date, but we were too busy making money to look outside the cocoon of the Beltway in which we worked. The only time it came up as a serious conversation was at a partners' meeting which I now attended. Cory asked Marc what he thought of the race and who should AMASS folks support. Marc's answer surprised us all.

"You know, my brother Anthony worked for many years for Harry Connard. Mr. Connard offered him a job after Anthony was released from the army. Anthony had been a POW and wasn't in very good shape, mentally or physically. He was always very good to Anthony, so while I don't think much of him as a candidate, I do feel I owe him a certain amount of allegiance." Marc drifted off. The rest of us said nothing.

EIGHT

CUTTER

In late April, The Flash stuck her head into my office and said, "Cutter, there's a call on line two you need to take."

"Who is it?"

"The CDC."

"This is Cutter Williams. How may I help you?"

"Mr. Williams, my name is Dr. Larry Gerstner with the Center for Disease Control. I'm the director of epidemiology for the Center and I could use your help."

"Certainly. What can we do for you?"

"Several months ago you spoke with Drs. Hoy and Frye in our administrative office and I believe offered a service which provides for the tracking of employees. Is that correct?"

"Well, Dr. Gerstner, that's part of it. It is actually designed as a manpower efficiency tool which collects all the data about an employee, from classification and salary to skill sets to background information. It also contains a component which provides for locating an employee at any given time using GPS technology. In short, the system allows an employer to maximize the efficient use of manpower by making sure the right person with the right skills is in the right place at the right time doing the right tasks. It additionally provides the means for an organization to measure its efficiency against industry standards. Does that all make sense?"

"It does. But what I am most interested in is the ability to track individuals."

"Your employees?"

"No. Actually we're looking for a way to track the spread of a disease with the goal of more quickly identifying and containing any potential epidemic outbreak. We think your system may allow us to get real time information which would lead us to more quickly ascertain how a disease is contracted and how it spreads. Do you think that's possible?"

"I would think so," I told him.

Dr. Gerstner went on, "What are the limitations on the number of individuals the system can keep track of?"

"Theoretically, the only limitation is the amount of server space available. But that's only a logistical problem. We can add however many servers you would require."

"With backup capability?"

"Yessir."

"I understand your company had offered this service for the CDC employees for free." Before I could respond he added, "But that won't be necessary. We have the funding to pay for it, assuming there is no charge until we use a slot. Is that okay?"

I smiled. "Yessir, that's how it works. No charge for the set up or the capability, only for actual individuals entered into the system."

Dr. Gerstner was quiet for a while and then said, "Get your technical people together and come see us. As soon as possible."

Now I grinned. "Would next Tuesday be soon enough?" I tried not to let my grin show through in my voice.

"Perfect. See you then."

Tuesday morning, The Flash, Julie Barney, Julie's assistant Mary

Beth Irelan and I flew to Atlanta. At the airport we were greeted by two uniformed gentlemen who whisked us into a huge black SUV with FEMA stenciled in discreet letters on the side. The Flash turned to me once we were stowed away in the cavernous back seat and asked, "I thought we were meeting with the CDC. What's with the FEMA thing?"

"Don't know, but I'd guess we're going to find out."

Thirty minutes later we were whisked out of the car and into CDC headquarters where we were greeted by Dr. Gerstner personally. He was not at all what I expected. I figured the doc would be a gray haired geriatric. This guy was maybe mid-thirties, tall, lean and ginger haired. And judging from the reaction of my three comrades, he must have been extremely good looking. KC and Mary Beth just stared; Julie grinned and blushed. Introductions were made and we followed the doc upstairs to his office, Julie close enough she could have had her hand in his pocket.

Once we were seated in his conference room, Dr. Gerstner laid out what he needed. "As I told Mr. Williams," he started and I interrupted with "Call me Cutter." He furrowed his brow and asked, "Are you a doctor?"

"No. What makes you think that?"

"I know a couple of surgeons called Cutter and I just wondered." He told us pretty much what he had told me on the phone. Julie and Mary Beth did their dog and pony show, the ridiculously technical presentation of the bells and whistles of AMASS's secret sauce. As always, The Flash remained alert to make sure we didn't lose our audience as was wont to happen with administrators. We didn't. In fact the good doctor seemed as taken with Julie as she was with him.

After they finished, he asked, "So does AMASS provide the tracking chips?"

KC took over, "No, but we have several suppliers we can direct you to, depending on what kind of GPS chip you think you may need. Some are low cost, such as a small chip which can be affixed to a name badge or ID card; others are more complex and can store more data on the chip itself. The most expensive, though I would guess you would have no need for that kind, are the chips which are embedded under the skin. Those are mostly used for tracking combat personnel."

"I see," Dr. Gerstner said and then turned his attention to Julie. "Ms. Barney, I followed most of what you were saying about the technical aspects of this system, but can you put into layman's terms exactly how this makes an organization more efficient?"

Julie blushed, again, and said, "Please, call me Julie. I'll try to…"

"Okay, Julie," he interrupted, "if you'll call me Larry," and he flashed a smile obviously meant to charm. It worked.

"Okay, Larry," she stammered and continued her explanation. "It's like the old business adage. It gets the right people on the bus, gets them in the right seat and gets them all facing forward, hopefully singing the same tune. And the wrong people off the bus."

I felt myself laugh, though it came out more as a derisive snort. The doc raised his eyebrows and Julie blushed even more deeply, almost crimson. "Sorry," I said, "but that was something a mayor I worked for once said and within a day he managed to drive the bus off a cliff. When they finally cleared away all the carnage, everybody on the bus was unemployed and several lives were ruined." I paused, then added, "But Julie's right. Used properly, AMASS's tool will help an organization maximize its resources. Is there any other information we can provide? References?"

The doc again turned to Julie and spoke. "Let me think about all this for a couple of hours and talk to my staff. Then maybe we could go over anything additional, perhaps over dinner? Would that work?"

Before Julie could respond, Mary Beth piped up with, "Sure. We could do that. Just let us know what to bring." She grinned.

"Uh, Mary Beth," The Flash said, "I don't think Dr. Gerstner meant all of us. I think he was talking to Julie." Julie continued her scarlet display and Larry continued to smile.

Mary Beth looked distraught and mumbled, "Oh. Sorry."

The Flash, Mary Beth and I had dinner early and went our separate ways, my way being via the hotel lobby bar. I watched the Braves clobber my Cubs and went to bed. I got up early, like 6:00 am, to go for a run through the Emory University campus. As I left the hotel, Julie was coming in, in the same clothes she had worn to dinner. I smiled and waved, she blushed yet again and stared at her feet. "Everything okay?" I asked, trying not to smile too broadly.

"Yes. Fine. I have to hurry, though. Larry, er, Dr. Gerstner wants to meet with Mary Beth and me at nine to talk to his staff. He said you don't have to come if you don't want to, and to let you know this is a done deal." She finally looked at me, beaming.

"Well done," I told her and squeezed her shoulder as a way of reassuring her I wouldn't rat her out to her father. "Tell Larry you guys can wrap things up. The Flash will stay in case CDC needs anything official. I'll see you back in D.C." I finished my run, went back to the hotel and called to see if I could get the next plane out of Atlanta Hartsfield.

I had to rush to get to the airport for my noon flight. I was the last one on the plane, we taxied out to the runway and sat for twenty minutes waiting to take off. We then taxied back to the gate and were deplaned. Mechanical problem of some sort. I had three hours to kill before I could get another flight, so I called the office and got Marc and Cory on the phone, reported on our meetings (without sharing the personal contribution Julie had made) and told them I would see them the next day. Marc was in one of his expansive and upbeat moods. He spent ten minutes telling me how great I was. When Marc left the room, Cory picked up the handset and said, "You can tell Marc is in a manic phase right now, but his mood has been all over the charts. The asshole Brandon finally showed up and whatever he had to tell Marc made Marc awfully happy. But I doubt it will last, so get your butt back here soonest."

"Will do. See you tomorrow."

I wandered down Concourse A to the first bar I could find. It's the Great American Airport Pastime, drinking. I found a seat at the bar, next to a young man dressed in seersucker shorts, flip flops and a tee shirt which read "Howard's Pub", my favorite bar on Ocracoke. He was sporting a tan and wearing sunglasses on top of his head. My guess was he was returning from spring vacation, but then again I have always been Captain Obvious. He looked up and smiled, said, "Hi," and returned to the book he was reading. I ordered a beer and was given a choice between huge or huger. I took huger.

I looked at the book the kid was reading and had to smile. He was reading the first Cutter book Barney had written. I asked him if he liked the book. He bobbed his head and said, "Beach novels and airport bars. Two of my favorite things. Kinda sounds like a Jimmy Buffett song, huh?"

"Is it any good?" I asked him.

"It's okay. Love the writing. The main character is kind of an asshole, but in a funny way, you know." He put his hand out and said, "I'm Peter. A friend of my dad's wrote the book. Kinda neat, knowing an author and all."

Small fucking world, it is. I shook his hand and said, "Winston. Nice to meet you."

"No kidding? The asshole in this book is named Winston. That's funny."

"Well, Peter, it's a funny world." He returned to reading and his beer, occasionally laughing at something he read. I returned to my beer and thought about the Cutter kid in the book. Things had seemed so important back then. So life shattering. Now I couldn't even conjure up the feelings from that time, those events. Some things had turned out better than I had ever imagined they could be, some things worse. Just as I was deciding things were in fact pretty good, news broke on the TV over the bar that three more of the presidential candidates were dropping out of the race after yesterday's primaries.

On the Democratic side, only Vice President Breiner and the liberal senator from California remained, and the senator's chances were waning quickly. On the Republican side, two previous front-running candidates had withdrawn after catastrophic showings in all five of the primaries. Both had been eliminated by the great political leveler, the internet. Photos of the ultra-conservative governor with a naked escort had appeared the week before, along with accusations of marital infidelity. So much for the Family Values candidate. I didn't see his departure as any loss at all. What was distressing was the senator from Ohio, the smartest and most moderate Republican running, was also out, having been accused of providing classified information to agents of Iran. As much as he denied it, he could not shake the accusations because of emails allegedly sent from his private email address. He finished dead last in all five races. Apparently, accusations of treason still ranked lower than illicit sex.

That left just three Republicans in the race. Most worrisome was the clear leader in terms of numbers of delegates was Harry Connard. It wasn't that he was doing such a fine job. In fact, he continued to insult everyone and stir up hatred in his speeches. It was that his opponents kept being killed off by bad press and rumors. It was plain weird, but I went from thinking things were okay in my life to being concerned about the country. Unusually civic minded of me. Still, Christ in a hand basket, scary.

NINE

CUTTER

I got back to D.C. just in time to take over the reins of parenthood from Sandy. She was leaving with Congresswoman Buday for a two-week tour of the congresswoman's home state, Iowa. Buday was the sole Democratic representative in the state and, like every representative, up for reelection. And like every Democrat, very worried about holding her seat. I guess I hadn't been paying much attention (shocking, I know) but apparently Sandy had won the congresswoman's favor as not only a policy geek, but also as a political advisor. At any rate, they were doing a series of town halls across the district and Sandy was orchestrating the whole shebang. The kids were, of course, happy for the change, not because I am a better parent, but because I'm easier to manipulate and don't make them do the stuff they are supposed to do. We settled in for fifteen days of pizza and ice cream and movies and video games.

My first day back to work I briefed the partners on the deal with the CDC and Cory pointed out somehow I had failed to tell them the CDC was going to pay for the service. Marc seemed happy, though not surprised, Cory and the two silent partners were elated. At least both Norman and Lowry smiled, which I took for elation. The timing seemed perfect to ask them if I could take a couple of weeks of working from home. No one had a problem with that, so I grabbed all my stuff and headed back home. I reacquainted myself with being a full-time dad and doing housework. It didn't take many days of the sole responsibility of taking Jordan and Livingston to school and preschool, running to the grocery store and drug store, picking up the kids and delivering them to lessons or sports practices, fixing meals, doing laundry and the endless cleaning of the kitchen to decide I couldn't be a stay at home or single dad. What made it worse, both kids seemed lots more interested in spending time with their friends than with me. Ingrates.

About ten days into our bachelordom, I had just gotten both the kids down for the count (at 11:00, way, way past their mother-imposed bed times) when my cell phone chirped.

"Hello?"

"Cutter, how the hell are you? What are you up to these days? Where are you? How are the kids and Sandy? We all miss you. Miss you."

I finally recognized the voice from the staccato delivery and upbeat smile behind the words—none other than Hammond Eggleston, mayor of Columbus, Colorado. Better known as Ham and Eggs. One of my all-time favorite people. "I'm great, Mr. Mayor. Good to hear your voice."

"Yours too, Son, yours too."

I'm not going to go into Ham and Eggs and my history. Ole J. Woodburn Barney covered that pretty well in the second book he wrote about me. Suffice it to say, he was one of those rare people who both enriched and entertained your life. I will always count him as a dear friend. "So to what do I owe the honor of a phone call from someone as esteemed as the Mayor of Columbus?"

"I need you to do me a favor, Son. A favor."

"Anything for you, Mr. Mayor. You just name it."

"Well, Hugh Stalter and the rest of the parks commission and I, think we never gave you a proper thanks for how you helped us here." I was actually a little shocked by his statement. My memory was I'd pretty much fucked up my run in Columbus. You can read Barney's book and decide for yourself. Ham and Eggs continued, "We're reopening Riverside Park next month and Hugh and I want you to be our special guest. Not sure if you read about it, the Jacob Matthew Cup was a huge success and folks around here are pretty pumped up to celebrate that and to get their park back open. Big to-do. Big."

Of course I had read about it, in fact, I'd watched enough of it on TV to get to see how the improvements to the park had turned out. "Sure, Your Honor. I'd love to come. But no thanks are needed. I'll be there if it will be low key."

"Sure, Son. Sure. Just as long as you are there. I'll have my assistant email you your tickets and hotel reservation. You're in the Founders Hotel. Hope that's okay. Nice hotel. Has a bar and restaurant. You'll like it." It was the best hotel in town. Though it contained a few bad memories, I figured what the hell and agreed.

A few days later Sandy got home, exhausted. She told me the trip had been a big success and Congresswoman Buday was quite pleased with how it had gone. She basically slept for three days and then got back into the swing of running our house. By running, I mean telling us all what to do and when and how to do it. Though she seemed strangely quiet and a little withdrawn.

I went back to working at the office where my day consisted mostly of signing papers and watching the money roll in. The only hiccup was when I returned, Julie was nowhere to be found. I asked Cory and he scowled and told me to ask Marc. So I did. Marc told me Dr. Gerstner had called and asked if Julie could be assigned as the on-site AMASS rep to the CDC and he had approved it. I explained to him she was way too valuable to send into the field and he snapped at me that it was his decision and to work around it. I figured Gerstner had just wanted to get laid more often, but I wasn't going to fight with Marc about it. I promoted Mary Beth.

Mid-June I flew to Columbus, Colorado for the park reopening. I was surprised how much I missed the mountains. And the dry air. Hugh and Ham and Eggs met me for dinner at the Aspen Ridge Brewery, and we spent several hours and many beers reminiscing and catching up on each other's lives. The next morning, I grabbed a cab and rode out to Riverside Park. The place was packed and I joined the throng of mostly smiling people and toured all the new facilities. Around noon we were all herded into the new performance hall. I stood at the back to watch all the dignitaries speechify. Anonymous.

As the president of city council introduced the mayor, I sensed a person standing close behind my left shoulder. There was a light touch on the back of my upper arm and a voice said, "Hey, Stranger." I turned and looked down into huge brown eyes beneath a pixie cut of shiny black hair. It took me a second to put it all together. She had cut off her long hair and lost weight, but Rachel Red Cloud was still as beautiful as ever, if not more so.

"Rachel," I more or less stammered, "you look tremendous. How are you? Why aren't you up there with the other dignitaries, taking bows and being feted?" Rachel had been my number two when I was the parks director here and was the current parks director. Very smart, very capable and undyingly loyal. And did I mention beautiful?

"That's for the politicians. Besides, Hugh told me you were here and I wanted to see you." She stopped and looked around. "Is she here?" I knew by the inflection who the "she" was—Sandy.

"Nope. She's too important for this kind of stuff. And she wasn't really the hero of the day, either, was she?" I smiled.

"So will you take me to dinner?" Rachel asked.

"Of course. It would be my pleasure." With that, she kissed me on the cheek, whirled and quickly made her way to the stage just as she was being introduced by Mayor Eggleston. She made a short speech thanking, by name, all of the elected officials and sponsors of the Jake (as the Jacob Matthews Cup was known) for returning Riverside Park to its former glory.

She closed by pointing back towards where I was standing and added, "Cutter Williams? Cutter, would you please raise your hand?" I did as told and she told everyone, "Cutter was the director who came up with the idea for hosting the Jake and made all this possible. Would you all please give him a hand?" There was the obligatory applause and I blushed and shuffled my feet. I have to admit, it was pretty nice. I made a mental note to accuse her of embarrassing me and to buy her a bottle of champagne. After the speeches concluded and everyone made a beeline to the bars and hors d'oeuvres, Rachel found me and told me she would meet me at The Pioneer, the very nice restaurant in my hotel. We agreed on 7:00 pm.

She was wearing a classic little black dress that had full length sleeves with wrist to shoulder slits held together with three ties each. High heels and a turquoise necklace. She looked stunning and I told her so. And apologized for my jeans and my worn blue blazer. Then again, the only reason anyone would look at me was to try to figure out why such a woman was with a dorky guy. The *maître d'* spent an inordinate amount of time hovering over her after we were seated and we could only be rid of him by suggesting he bring us cocktails. Airplane gin and tonic for me; scotch on the rocks for Rachel.

"So tell," I ordered. "New look to match your position?" While Rachel had always been beautiful, when I had worked with her she mostly wore plain CPAish suits or jeans and western shirts.

She smiled (and I think blushed, though it was hard to tell) and said, "Actually, I wore this for you." It was my turn to blush.

Our conversation turned to the safety of mundane topics. How staff was doing, what was going on in the parks department, city officials, people we knew in common. Rachel filled me in on how the Jake preparation had gone and all about the event. She asked about Sandy and the kids. I told her about Sandy's work for Congresswoman Buday and all about the kids' lives. I asked her about her daughter Elena and her husband, The Chief. He wasn't a real chief, or at least I didn't think he was, but that's how Rachel always referred to him.

"Elena's doing great. She's off to college this fall. In your area, in fact. She got a scholarship from the tribal council to attend Georgetown. The Chief is gone. Left for parts unknown." The last she said without any emotion. I must have shown real surprise by my expression.

"I know. I was surprised as well," she added. "He just came home one night and announced he was leaving. Said I could have everything, but that I was on my own." Still no emotion in her voice, though her eyes dampened. I waited. "So I cut my hair, went to the gym and bought a new wardrobe. Turns out I don't miss him as much as I should."

I always feel awkward when people open up like this to me. I'm never sure what I should do, so I fell back to my standard reaction. I got up, walked to her side of the table and offered her a hand and hugged her when she stood. I held her for a minute or so. She let me. Then the fantasies I had had about her flooded back and I pushed her away gently. She smiled and said quietly, "Thank you, Cutter." She excused herself and went to the restroom. When she returned we carried on as if we were old colleagues just renewing an acquaintance.

After dinner I convinced her to join me for a nightcap, just one, in the hotel's lobby bar. I asked her what her plans were. What I had meant was what her plans were for the department now that Riverside was back in operation. As in, what new big glorious ideas did she have at work?

"Gee, Cutter, I don't know," she answered, shaking her head. "I suppose when Elena leaves I'll find a smaller place, maybe just rent.

My family, my mom and brothers, all live in the Four Corners area, so I have no family around here. I'm not sure if I'll stay with the department or maybe look around for something else." Her gaze shifted off to somewhere in the future.

You can ask pretty much anyone and they'll tell you that thinking before speaking is not one of Winston Weller Williams' strong suits. Before I knew it, "So why don't you come work for me?" was coming out of my mouth. "You'd be close to Elena, the work isn't all that difficult, and the pay is pretty good." Somewhere in the back of my mind, I knew it would be okay with Marc. He had told me on more than one occasion he practiced Tom Landry's philosophy, "Hire the best talent available. Don't worry about what position they'll play. Good people will make a place for themselves." And Rachel Red Cloud was plenty talented. And smart. And did I mention beautiful?

"What?" was her only reply. I repeated my offer.

"Why would I want to do that? I don't know anything about what your company does."

"I don't either," I assured her. "But you don't need to. We have lots of techie folks who do the real work. We just herd the cats. Look, you just admitted there is nothing to keep you here. No family. Some bad memories, I'm sure. Doesn't sound like you're all that excited about the parks work anymore. At least come visit us and meet the AMASS folks. Think of it as a free vacation to D.C.." I gave her my best pretty-please-with-sugar-on-it smile.

"Let me think about it. Come out to the office tomorrow and I'll buy you some lunch. You can say hi to folks."

"Okay."

We had lunch the next day and she agreed to come to D.C.. I called Marc to warn him what I had done. His response was that it was a great idea. Having a Native American on staff would open up more doors for the company for contracts.

Christ in a hand basket, what was I thinking?

As I suspected, Marc and the other partners loved her and made her an offer she couldn't refuse. She would start out helping Cory with the finances and help me as might be needed. They agreed to put her up in the company apartment for six months and she was to start in late summer when she brought her daughter back east to college. The only negatives were Mayor Eggleston called me and chewed me out, good naturedly, for stealing his most valuable player and Sandy, who had worked with Rachel, didn't greet the news with enthusiasm. *C'est la vie.*

TEN

MOTHER

Brandon Jones showed up at the offices of AMASS about fifteen months after Captain Anthony Payton had supplanted his twin brother Marc as CEO of the company. He demanded to see Marc and was told since he didn't have an appointment, he could make one for later. He scowled at Barbara Belville, muttered "bitch" under his breath and punched a number into his cell phone. Almost immediately, Marc appeared at the reception desk and apologized to Brandon for keeping him waiting. He also scowled at Barbara and took Brandon by the arm and led him back to his office. Barbara muttered "prick" under her breath.

"Mr. Payton, Mother has a request."

"Brandon, I have a question. If you supposedly work for me, why is it Mother only talks to you and you are always giving me orders? I want to hear directly from Mother if she needs something."

"I'm sorry, Sir, but I can only do as I am instructed. I would suggest you do the same."

"Fine," Marc spat out. "What the fuck does Mother want now?"

"She needs for AMASS to get its program into the systems of a couple of federal agencies."

Marc stared at Brandon. "What the hell do you think we're doing now? I swear to God, Brandon, you must have screwed up the orders. I'll talk to Mother myself. I'm ordering you to give me her contact information."

Brandon's face flushed with anger and he hissed between his teeth, "Anthony, I suggest you do exactly what I tell you to do. You met Mother, twenty years ago, when she hired you. If she wanted you to have her contact information, she would have given it to you. Listen and listen carefully. I speak for Mother. You have an arrangement with Mother. You don't do as I ask, you are in forfeit of your agreement with Mother. I assume you still remember what such forfeiture would entail, don't you?" Marc said nothing. "Well, do you?"

Marc softly answered, "Yes."

"Good. By the end of the year before the next presidential election, Mother wants your program in the government's Center for Disease Control and the Federal Emergency Management Agency. If possible, also get it into USAID, though that one isn't as critical as the other two."

"But what if they don't want it?"

Brandon sighed. "I don't really give a rat's ass what they want or don't want. Just do it." He shook his head. "Anthony, Marc, whoever you are, if this is too big for you, and I should warn you it's going to get a lot bigger, maybe we should just terminate your contract now." Before Marc could respond, Brandon pulled a Glock G28 from a shoulder holster and aimed it at Marc's nose.

Marc threw his hands up in front of his face just as someone knocked on his door. Barbara called through the door and asked if everything was alright. Marc hoarsely answered, "Yeah. Fine. Everything's okay. We'll be done in a minute." He patted his hands downward and Brandon lowered the gun to his side but did not return it to its holster. Marc continued quietly, "I can handle it, Asshole. I was doing this before you were your father's erection." Brandon smiled and slipped the gun under his jacket.

"What can you tell me about what is happening?" Marc asked.

"Mother is taking a special interest in the next presidential election, in fact, hopes to have some influence on its outcome. If all goes her way, we will need to have some of our people already in place. And some of our programs, including yours. AMASS is very critical to our success. It's why you are here; it's why you have been carried in relative luxury for twenty years. I'll do everything I can to help you, but I'm sure you can manage what Mother asks."

"How far up does this go on Mother's side?"

"All the way up. All the way to Mother's big boss."

"The Russian President?"

Brandon smiled and nodded his head. "Yep. The time has come. We have the means, we have the technology, we have mastered the power of the internet, and America has become lazy, fat and most importantly, stupid. One hundred years and who would have thought that instead of spies and armies and nuclear bombs the best weapon we would ever have would be the self-imposed ignorance of the population of the greatest democracy ever. Unbelievable when you think about it."

It was Marc's turn to smile. "Not unbelievable in the least. Reagan turned the country into a profit center for the rich. Money has become everything. The rich need to keep the poor stupid to separate them for their money. Pretty funny when you think about it. Reagan is the president credited with bringing down the Soviet

Union. Makes a guy believe in karma." He paused, then "Speaking of money, I'll probably need a bit of a cash infusion into the company to staff up for the additional work. I assume I can count on Mother for a loan, say quarter of a million?"

"No problem, but you probably should get someone in to drum up business. No one would believe that FEMA and the CDC would just fall into your lap. And don't hire someone who knows a lot about the federal government, just to be safe. Don't waste Mother's money."

"Tell Mother she has nothing to worry about. It would be helpful to know what she is going to use the AMASS program for, so see if you can get any more information."

"Will do, Boss," Brandon answered, without a hint of irony. He buttoned his jacket to conceal his weapon, turned and walked out the door of Marc's office and out onto the street with no more conversation. Not surprisingly, Marc didn't hear from Brandon for another eighteen months.

Two weeks later, Cory was waiting at the front door when Marc arrived at work. Before Marc could remove his coat, Cory pounced. "Marc, I'm not sure what's going on, but $280,000 just showed up in our account, a transfer from a bank in godforsaken Toledo, Ohio. You got any idea why it's there?"

"Oh, shit, Cory. I'm sorry. I forgot to tell you. I decided if we are going to grow, we need to expand our capabilities and then take an aggressive approach to business development, so I arranged for a loan. I figured it'd be a help to you if I did the financing. Got a hell of a deal on the money too. Trust me on this. We're gonna get into the big time."

Cory shook his head but said, "You're the boss. Think you should tell Norman and Lowry? They're your partners too, you know."

"Nah. They'd only worry. And Norman's wife would sit on him and slap the sides of his head. Besides, I signed for this loan personally. Worst thing happens, the business dies and I lose my house. It ain't gonna happen." Cory decided to update his *resumé*. Just in case.

Marc continued, "I'll take care of finding us a business development type. You put Norman on finding us a couple of hot shot developers. And tell him I want them to be female. More likely to stick around. And cheaper. But don't let him hire them until you okay it. *Capiche?*"

Cory nodded his head and asked, "Anything else?"

"Yeah, I don't think being in Davenport is gonna work for us anymore. We'll keep a small office here, but find us an office in the D.C. area. And get us some housing there."

ELEVEN

CUTTER

Summer started and we switched gears, both at home and at work. Jordan went from school to camps, week in and week out. I thought maybe Sandy was overscheduling her, that maybe she should be allowed to just be a kid some during the summer. Hang out in the neighborhood, bike to the store and swimming pool, build forts with her friends, catch fireflies, and come home for dinner, tired, hungry and happy. Apparently, I was wrong. Sandy scheduled our baby girl into a dozen day camps and a couple more overnighters. Horse camp, dance camp, wilderness camp, guitar camp, cooking camp (okay, so I could get on board with that one), math camp and others I couldn't name, though there was probably a princess camp and be mean to your little brother camp in there somewhere. The two big shocks were Jordan was all for it and I had been named the designated dropper offer and picker upper.

I couldn't really make much of an argument against being drafted. Summer was a slow time operationally for us at AMASS and Congresswoman Buday's campaign was going into full swing. Sandy warned me she would be spending most of the summer and fall in Iowa. I was a little surprised by my reaction. Other than being a little pissed I was shouldering most of the parental duties, I really didn't care that much. Sort of a summer vacation.

Early June political primaries finished off what had become foregone conclusions, as inexplicable and undesirable as they were.

June's Super Tuesday (in a seemingly unending series of Super Tuesdays) put both Vice President Breiner and Harry Connard over the number of delegates needed for nomination. There were some cries from the moderate Republican faction to convince delegates to switch votes and support another candidate because they believed Connard would ruin their party. The Democrats were nothing short of ecstatic about his nomination. They knew it guaranteed them a win in November. Except for those fringe and disenfranchised voters who got Connard nominated, the huge majority of voters would see him for what he was—an egotistical windbag and hatemonger completely unfit to be president. Even Connard's choice as a running mate thrilled the Democrats. Mike Shilling was a former judge who gained fame from a case in which he sent two gay couples to jail for, well, for being gay. The convictions were both overturned on appeal, but the judge was embraced by the Christian right. He was at his core a bible-thumping intellectual light weight. Except for the religious zealots he brought to the campaign, he had very little constituency of his own.

Connard's rallies continued to draw large, vocal and sometimes violent crowds. Protesters were quickly shouted down or physically attacked and the press began running comparisons of Connard political rallies to Hitler political rallies. Many of us worried, not about the potential of Connard being elected, but about the fear and hatred which were becoming widespread and the violence which accompanied it. But press coverage only appeared to make people want more of him. Love or loathe him, everyone wanted to see The Connard on TV and the internet. It was almost like he was a caricature of an old time politician. He would take both sides of an issue, he would make promises which no one could keep, he would lie and then lie about lying. If you tried to find his stance on anything, you would only get more frustrated.

By comparison, James Breiner looked like the quintessential elder statesman. He tried to stay above the fray, issued plans for programs and legislation, and closed the distance between his actual liberal position and the middle of the road. Spoke with intelligence to the intelligent. Reminded folks of his pro-choice stance, his pro-environment stance, his pro-children stance and his pro-business stance. The early polls had him leading by over twenty points, 58% to 37% among likely voters. His numbers among women voters was incredibly high, 65% versus 32%. Minority voters were close to the numbers for women. His numbers fell a little right after the Republican convention, but recovered after his formal nomination, when he chose as his running mate an African American female.

Ten days after Breiner's nomination, a video surfaced of him being interviewed by a reporter from the *Bible Belt Bulletin*, an ultra-conservative newsletter serving a group of right wing churches banded together to influence elections toward what they called "A More Godly America". In the video, Breiner could be heard saying, quite distinctly, "I do not favor pro-choice." The article in the newsletter said while doing the interview, Breiner "was touched by the hand of God and was led to righteousness." The clip of the interview and the article, which urged all real Christians to vote for

Breiner, flooded the news cycle and bounced from social network to social network. Breiner, of course, denied it, said he had explicitly told the reporter he did favor pro-choice and the clip was somehow adulterated. Since 80% of the internet denizens did not know the meaning of "adulterated", his claim was quickly dismissed and his support from women fell to less than 50% overnight.

Breiner went on the offensive and started holding pro-choice rallies in all of the swing states. The voters he had picked up from the religious right quickly defected, but he was unable to recover many of the women's votes already lost. All the while, Candidate Connard continued his rallies, preaching his litany of bringing jobs back to America for Americans. He was spending untold millions for advertising, apparently from his own coffers. By mid-September Connard had built a 5% lead in the polls. Nonetheless, we told ourselves voters would come to their senses when they got into the booth. Of course that was before two women came forth and claimed to have had affairs with Breiner years before and one of them aborted a pregnancy from the affair. Coincidently, she worked for the Russian embassy in Washington. Connard's attack ads reached a fever pitch.

As promised, Sandy pretty much disappeared from our radar screen by late summer. Breiner's substantial problems had begun to infect the entire party, including Congresswoman Buday. Sandy did manage to call the kids every day, but when we talked she seemed distracted and distant. She was obviously under a lot of pressure because at the end of August Buday's lead in the polls had disappeared. She told me she probably wouldn't be home for at least a month, maybe longer. I reminded her September was our busiest month for booking new business and I would have to spend a lot of time on the work side of my life. I was surprised and pissed by her response. "Look, Winston, I'm sure AMASS can do fine with you spending a little less time at the office since all you guys are selling is bullshit anyway. What I'm doing is important to the future of the country." I actually couldn't argue with her, but still, it stung to hear her say it. She went on, "Besides, you have Rachel there now and she can do anything you can do. And the kids love her, so she can help with them."

I offered an exquisite retort, "Fine. Whatever."

In fact, Sandy was right. Rachel Red Cloud could do anything I could do, plus things I couldn't. And the kids loved her. Jordan told me once she wanted to be beautiful like Rachel when she grew up. I urged her not to share that with her mother. Rachel arrived Labor Day weekend, moved into the AMASS apartment and spent Labor Day grilling out with Jordan, Livingston and me. It was like no time had passed for her and the kids in the twenty months since they had seen her. It all felt comfortable and easy.

Work was a madhouse all September long. As Marc had predicted, every federal agency hustled to spend whatever money was left in their coffers and we were there to help them do it. I shouldn't have been, but I was surprised how quickly Rachel was able to jump into the fray, even joining Marc on a sales call to the Office of Budget and Management where, according to Marc, her expertise in numbers sealed the deal. In the weekly partners' meeting, Marc congratulated me for hiring her. As always, whenever he praised me, I rubbed my fingers together indicating I wanted more compensation. He grinned and told me he had given that raise to Rachel. Three weeks into the job and already she had gotten an increase. Typical Marc. Typical Rachel.

At the height of sales madness, Mary Beth came to me and told me she thought there might be some kind of glitch with our software. She explained it to me, but with technical jargon. I'm pretty much like the dog Baily when I hear it. What I say: "Good dog, Baily. Let's go for a walk. Come on, Baily. You'll like it. You can sniff other dogs' butts and chase a squirrel or two. Let's go Baily." What the dog hears: "Blah, blah Baily. Blah blah blah blah. Blah blah, Baily. Blah, blah blah blah blah blah blah blah blah. Blah blah, Baily." I asked Mary Beth to put it into layman's terms.

"Cutter, you know how the system is set up to pay us, right?" The look on my face told her I didn't. She sighed and went on, "Each time a client adds an employee to be tracked, the system assigns the employee a unique ID number. Those numbers are used only once and will forever identify that individual and that agency. Once the employee is gone, the number is retired permanently. The assignment of those numbers is what generates our billing. A client adds ten employees, the system assigns them each a number and tells billing to charge the client for ten slots. Understand?"

"Yeah, I get it. So what's the problem?"

"I was live tracking the CDC installation to make sure it was functioning okay, just like I do with all of our contracts. Numbers would show up as being assigned, but those numbers would not kick over to the billing side. They just seemed to disappear. After it happened the second time, I noted one of the numbers to see if it was still available or not. It was gone from the system, retired, but with no information."

I asked her, "What does that mean? Are they using the number or not?"

"No. It's just gone."

"What do you think it means?"

"It could be the numbers are being generated automatically without input, but if that's the glitch, I can't find it. I called Julie Barney and asked her to look into it. She called back and told me it must be a problem on our end, but she doesn't think it's anything to worry about."

"You think we should be worried about it? I mean, Julie seems to have a good handle on things."

"I don't know. I just can't figure it out."

"Is it happening with any of our other clients?"

"It doesn't seem to have anything to do with any particular client. I just happened to notice it when I was tracking CDC."

"Well, Julie is there to watch over things, so let's not do anything right now."

"Okay. I just thought you should know."

Nonetheless, I figured I should let someone know, so during the next meeting I had with Marc, I brought it up. His face darkened and I was thinking maybe Mary Beth had found something important. Instead, Marc yelled at me. "Cutter, why the fuck do you bring this trivial crap to me? If Julie Barney says it's not a problem, it's not a problem. Unless of course you know more about software and programming than she does. Do you?" he practically hissed. I backed out of his office, almost secretly hoping it was a serious glitch and AMASS, and its CEO, would get screwed.

We got through September and booked about a dozen new clients, mostly on the military side. Since defense clients always seemed to require more hand holding, I enlisted Cory and The Flash to help me hire the new help we would need. Cory and the other partners drifted around the office with smiles on their faces and dollar signs in their eyes. By mid-October, Vice President Breiner had climbed out of his slump and was again ahead in the polls, which also seemed to lighten the spirits in the office. I have to admit, things were going pretty damned well for me. Good at work, the kids were doing well and were happy, Sandy had gotten to come home for a couple of weeks once Congresswoman Buday had reestablished her lead in the polls (though she would have to spend the last two weeks before the election in Iowa), Rachel and I got to spend lots of time together, and the weather had been beautiful enough for several rounds of golf with beers. Of course, the gods just hate seeing anyone as happy as I was.

November 8, Election Day, was an unofficial holiday at AMASS. The kids were staying with their visiting grandmother overnight and Sandy was in Iowa, so I worked in the morning and then convinced Rachel to join me for food and drink and to watch the returns in the evening. My contact at FEMA, Ellen Thordarson, had scored me a couple of tickets (face value $50 but Ellen assured me they had been provided free to them, so I didn't have to worry about impropriety, not that I would have anyway) to the Elkhorn Room in the Teddy and the Bully Bar. It was supposed to be a great place to watch the returns. Plus the ticket included all-you-can-eat bar bites and all-you-can-drink Moscow Mules, which oddly portended what was to come.

The weather was cold and rainy, the bane of the Democratic Party, not just in D.C. but along the entire East Coast. Rachel and I had lunch at Oyamel Cocina Mexicana on 7th Street NW (which she pronounced as very authentic) and then wandered down to the National Gallery and spent the entire afternoon meandering through the paintings and talking, mostly about her daughter Elena and my kids. It was obvious she missed her daughter, and as we stood in front of *Whistler's Symphony in White, No 1: The White Girl*, Rachel started to cry. The girl in the painting did remind me of Elena. I held her for a couple of minutes and as we continued our stroll, Rachel took my hand and held it. It felt perfectly natural.

We caught a cab up to the bar and were among the first to arrive. We grabbed a couple of seats with a good view of the television and settled in for the evening. The place was soon packed and the mood more somber than festive. Early exit polls were not going well for Breiner, who was very popular in D.C. circles. As the early returns started arriving, the mood went from somber to bitter. By midnight it was apparent Harry Connard had garnered enough electoral votes to become the next president of the United States. When the news channels made their announcement, the bar fell silent. Folks grabbed their coats and umbrellas and quietly made their way out onto the streets. Somehow Connard had won. What had looked like a lunatic campaign had reaped its reward.

Say what you will, the campaign had employed an absolutely brilliant strategy, one no one had ever figured out before. It was as if his campaign designer completely discarded traditional American thinking and replaced it with a strange combination of fascism, communism and oligarchy. He castigated the national press (the very same press which had made him a political superstar) and employed social media with a never-before-discovered acumen. He managed to use the anachronistic Electoral College to win with a minority. Of course, that had been done before, several times. The brilliant part was the minority coalition he had put together to accomplish it. And while I say "he", I mean whoever was running Harry's sideshow, since he never struck me, or anyone else for that matter, as being anywhere near smart enough to think of those things on his own. Yet, there it was, a coalition comprised of the greedy, the ignorant, bigots, ageists, racists, homophobes, misogynists, isolationists, skinheads, Nazis, the KKK, the Christian ISIS, the believers of Fox News and a wide assortment of psychopaths and sociopaths. And they would now be running the country.

Rachel and I took the yellow line back to Alexandria, and she suggested I use one of the spare bedrooms at the apartment to avoid driving out to the burbs and then right back in. I agreed. The presidential election day is a D.C. festive day. Generally speaking, half the town is happy with results, half isn't, but everyone celebrates that once again our system of democracy works. And, of course, that the bureaucracy slugs along unscathed. Tonight was different, especially for those on the Metro. Rich folks don't use the Metro. Only working stiffs like us and lots of government employees. The president-elect had promised to slash government waste by just outright eliminating hundreds of agencies and thousands of programs, mostly involving services for the young, the poor, the uneducated, the elderly, the less fortunate and the environment or those which regulated the negative impact the rich and their businesses could have on the rest of us. It was to be a feast and the middle and poorer classes were on the menu. Our fellow passengers relied on the government for their jobs or services and all knew they were in for a rough four years unless, as someone in the back of the car suggested, "Maybe someone will just kill the son of a bitch before the inauguration." There were a few laughs, but the mood remained dark. Rachel and I huddled together silently.

We got back to the apartment, the one I had lived in when I first arrived, and Rachel offered to make us scrambled eggs and bacon. It was the first thing in hours which sounded good. I made us a couple of Bloody Marys and we had a late night breakfast. After some discussion we decided AMASS and our jobs would probably be safe since we primarily serviced the Department of Defense. Rachel said goodnight, kissed me on the cheek, squeezed my shoulder and went to her room.

I opened the laptop to check on a couple of the races for Congress. I saw my old acquaintance in Colorado, Whitney Husz, had retained her seat, a good thing. I found the live feed from Congresswoman Buday's headquarters just in time to see her acceptance speech. Those two Congresswomen proved to be the exception. Many Democrats lost and now both the House and the Senate were under the control of Connard's party. It did not bode well. Michele Buday, still with the signature twinkle in her eyes, was gracious, accepted her opponent's concession and praised him for running a good campaign. Pure Iowa horseshit. She then invited her family and her staff to join her at the podium. Her husband and children stood on her right, Sandy immediately to her left, along with three or four other staffers.

Buday thanked her supporters with special mention of her husband and kids and then of Sandy. I felt really good about that. The congresswoman took Sandy's and her husband's hands and raised them high in the air as balloons dropped from the ceiling. The camera panned across the group and came to Sandy. She was not looking at either the camera or the congresswoman. She was, the word coming to me slowly, "gazing" at the tall young man to her left who held her hand triumphantly in the air. I'd seen that look before. It was the same one she had worn when she was with Clint Brandsgard and later with me. I knew what it meant. Christ in a hand basket. I didn't feel so good anymore.

TWELVE

CUTTER

Marc called a staff meeting first thing the next day and we all gathered and sat silently waiting for him, still stunned from last night's news. He finally bounced into the conference room, positively ebullient. We realized Marc felt a certain debt to the president-elect because he had helped Marc's brother, but Marc had also ranted about how surprised he was Connard was so openly racist. At one point Marc had even compared Connard to George Wallace.

"Good morning, troops," Marc smiled. "Everyone stay up too late watching the returns? Why so glum?"

A female voice from the back answered, "Because we now have a certifiable asshole for president."

A dark cloud passed over Marc's face, but just for a second, and his smile returned. "Oh, c'mon. It's not that bad. You know a president on his own can't do that much damage. Besides, he'll be good for the economy. Already this morning the Dow is up over 200 points. And he isn't even president yet. That said, we do need to take a proactive position. Cory will assign clients to each of the partners and senior staff. We need you each to take along the client rep and make a personal visit to see them. Every one of our clients. We want this to happen in the next week or so."

"To do what?" Lowry asked.

"To hold their hands, mostly. Listen to what they say about the upcoming changes; see if there is any way we can help. And I don't mean just with our software program. Ask if there is anything at all we can do for them. We need to gather as much information as we can about the general mood out there and bring it all together to see if we need to adjust our corporate strategy. Remember, we don't acquire contracts, we acquire clients. Find out how we can help and then we'll figure out how to do it." He paused. "Cory?"

Cory stood and made the assignments. I expected to be given the CDC and FEMA, but drew the Corps of Engineers and the IRS, along with Mary Beth. I was surprised Marc himself was going to visit CDC and FEMA, as well as OMB. He was taking Rachel with him.

We spent the rest of the day making appointments and booking travel. At least my travel would be by Metro so the kids wouldn't have to be on their own while Sandy finished up in Iowa. I was still pretty numb about what I'd seen on the live feed from Iowa last night, but instead of anger, it felt like it was just adding to the special cold place in my gut I had reserved for her. That might change when I saw her. The day seemed to drag on forever and I was bone tired by the time I picked up the kids at 5:30.

I took them out for pizza, then home to get them ready for the next day. By 8:30, we climbed into bed for story time. By 8:40, all three of us were asleep, Jordan on her mom's pillow and Livingston sprawled between us, limbs akimbo. We were still in those positions at 1:00 in the morning when Sandy came in. She woke us up, hugging and kissing the kids. Sandy grinned and laughed and bounced around the house, making everyone get up for hot chocolate and popcorn. The kids, of course, were all for a middle-of-the-night party. As the milk warmed for the hot chocolate, she changed into her PJs and then came over and gave me a big hug and a very suggestive kiss. My body returned both.

"Cutter, I have great news. The congresswoman just appointed me head of staff. It involves a lot more responsibility, but also a lot more money. And I'll probably be spending about one third of my time back in Iowa. I think we need to seriously consider hiring a live-in nanny/housekeeper/cook." Apparently my look was not one of excitement. She went on, "Oh, Cutter, this will be so good for us, for both of us. Michele even has a woman she wants us to hire, Maria Fuentes. Highly recommended. What do you think?" She continued to beam.

Maria Fuentes. Perfect. In the time-honored Washington tradition. Domestic help from an unidentified Latin American country, one who may or may not be completely legal, but is certainly cheap.

"Sure," I said, trying to sound more excited than I was. In fact, not having to worry about scurrying hither and yon would be a relief, but still. It just didn't sound properly parental. Sandy ran on about the election, the congresswoman, Iowa and her new job for another hour, until we put the kids back to bed in their own rooms. Not once did she mention any tall, attractive and younger coworker.

As soon as we got to our room, she stripped and jumped onto the bed. I felt somehow complicit in a deception, but it took no additional encouragement for me to join her. We didn't speak, we didn't kiss, we exchanged no affection. She climbed on me and, sorry, there is no other word for it, she fucked me. With passion and no emotion, if that makes sense. It didn't make sense to me—women just don't act this way. Afterwards, she said, "Good night," rolled over and was snoring within five minutes. I lay on my back and felt a deepening sense of loss.

Marc had been spot on about the visits to clients. Every one of them seemed pleased we took the time to come see them and to ask what, if anything, we could do to help with the transition. Most asked for small things, little things and most seemed to be very happy to learn Marc actually had a distant relationship with the new president. Then, like all of the federal government, we hunkered down to wait.

The timing was good in that we basically got to relax and enjoy the holidays, from Thanksgiving through New Year's. The Williams family packed up and drove to Iowa when Jordan's winter break began and stayed 'til the first week of January. We visited my extended family and Sandy's smaller one. The kids loved seeing the grandparents and cousins. Sandy spent most of the time on the phone, locked in a bedroom. I spent most of the time watching television which on a daily basis charted the president-elect's cabinet choices. They were mostly old white men who unabashedly vowed to disassemble the social service, education, housing, insurance, health, and environmental programs instituted over the previous 80 years. I have to admit I was a little surprised they didn't announce the rollback of civil rights legislation and women's suffrage. Maybe that was to come. Harry Connard might as well have gone on national television and quoted Kurt Russell in *Tombstone*, "Tell 'em I'm comin' and hell's comin' with me."

President Connard's inauguration was marred by protests, but the police bashed in a few heads and the protesters quickly retreated. The national news organizations tried to report on those events, but the reports were quickly dismissed as "fake news" by the new administration. Connard's staff appointments were, to a person, completely without government experience and most had been on the security staff of Connard International Resorts. Marc pointed out that had his brother lived he might very well be in the White House.

Over the next few months, as the new administration started to exert its power, many of our civilian clients began losing employees which of course negatively affected our billing. The only exceptions seemed to be the CDC and FEMA. Of course, we had given the service to FEMA and as of yet, the CDC was not using many slots. Cory expressed concern, but Marc waved him away, saying to wait, things would be fine.

Because our clients were in a state of turmoil, my life became a daily grind of listening to complaints and concerns and whines, most of which I could do nothing about. I had just gotten off the phone with the Army Corps of Engineers who said they were considering dropping our program unless we could reduce the cost when Rachel walked into my office. She needed a report from me which was overdue. It was one of those final straws. I erupted, "Goddamnit, Rachel, can't you see I've got real problems? You'll just have to wait for your fucking report." She actually shrank back from me, tears in her eyes, and I realized what I had done. I stammered, "Geez, I'm sorry. I didn't mean that. It's just been one of those days. All I want right now is to be left alone and have an airplane gin and tonic and some chocolate chip cookies." Rachel backed out of my office wordlessly. I felt terrible.

To make the day even darker, immediately afterwards Cory grabbed me and led me by the arm into Marc's office, telling me he needed me to listen to what he had to say. We closed the door and sat in front of Marc's desk.

"What?" Marc barked.

Cory thought for a couple of minutes, then asked, "Can you tell me what is going on with our accounts?"

"What do you mean?"

"You know goddamn well what I mean. You're moving all kinds of money through several partnership accounts, money which has nothing to do with AMASS."

Marc frowned. "Cory, it doesn't involve you. Don't worry about it. I have another temporary business interest and using my accounts here is just easier than setting up new ones. It's only for a short time. It's not a problem." His face darkened. "Got it?"

Cory flushed slightly and told Marc, "But in fact it does involve me. Those are partnership accounts and as you may remember, as CFO, it is MY name on them. That means I'M responsible for what goes on in those accounts, just as much if not more than you and the other partners. It's the IRS on MY ass if something is amiss. And frankly, Mr. Payton, to any IRS agent it would look a lot like money laundering." By this time Cory was deep red and almost shouting.

Marc lost it. "Listen, you little shit, this is MY company. You were a volunteer bartender when I picked your ass off the streets and you can just as easily go back there if you don't like the way I do things. I tell you it's okay and doesn't involve you, and that's all you need to know." He turned towards me. "And what the fuck are you doing here? This is none of your concern."

Before I could respond (thankfully, since I had no clue what I was doing there), Cory answered him. "I asked him to be here. Marc, I'm serious. You can't use AMASS accounts this way. We'll all be in trouble. The money shows up, when I try to figure out where it came from, it all leads to numbered accounts. On the surface, it looks very shady." Marc harrumphed and Cory went on, "Look, I'll set up another account you can use. It really isn't that big of a problem. I can keep your name off of it if that helps. Just don't fuck around with the company's standing. Please."

Marc waved the back of his hand at us and grunted, "Fine. Just do it. And not another word on this, understand?" He looked at me. "That goes for you too, Williams." Then back to Cory, "Now get the fuck out of my office." We turned to leave. "And call Brandon and tell him I need to see him RFN."

After we retreated, I asked Cory, "What was that all about?"

"I'm not sure. It's hinky and it worries me. I don't know what he's doing, but it feels wrong. You just don't go screwing around with the IRS, especially when most of your money comes from the federal government." He paused and thought for a minute, then said, "Don't worry about it. I'll fix it."

"You mean it's something I should worry about?"

"Yep, if I can't get it fixed." He turned and walked to his office.

Son of a bitch. I sat at my desk and pouted and spent the rest of the afternoon listening to both client and staff complaints and whines. The clock moved like it had been dipped in syrup and finally, mercifully, ticked to five. I pulled on my jacket and slouched out the door without saying a word to anyone. I got to my Wrangler and sitting on my seat was a small thermos and a large bag of Famous Amos chocolate chip cookies. The thermos was filled with an airplane gin and tonic. I have never felt more like a shit than I did at that moment.

I didn't come out of my funk. I managed to apologize to Rachel who forgave and forgot. Good thing, since she and the kids tended to be the bright spots in my life. Cory and Marc apparently settled their differences, but whether from internal or external forces, the office felt more on edge than ever before. It was quickly becoming a pain in the ass to go in. I needed a vacation, maybe a little Hatteras time. Absolute best part of working in D.C.—Hatteras was only five hours away.

"Hey, Cory, I'm gonna book a couple of weeks on the Outer Banks. Does it make any difference to you when I go? Or for that matter, do you and your girlfriend want to join us?"

"Actually, Cutter, I think one of us needs to be here at all times, and I'm already scheduled for vaca the first two weeks of July. But thanks for the invite."

"No problem. We'll go the end of July, first weeks of August. Where you going?"

Cory smiled and shook his head. "You're not gonna believe it. I'm doing a bucket list thing this summer. The guys and I are going to the Fiestas of San Fermin."

"Uh huh, that sounds exciting. Gonna wear a sombrero and drink margaritas, are you? Fun times."

His smile turned to a grin. "No, Asshole, not exactly. San Fermin is in Pamplona. Brett, Nolan and I are gonna run with the bulls."

I laughed. "Sure you are."

"No, really," he said, turning serious. "I've always wanted to do it and this is the year."

"Are you nuts? You could get killed. What's your girlfriend say about all this?"

"She loves it—she's getting a free trip to Spain."

I just shook my head. "Well, I want to hear all about it."

I booked my trip for the first two weeks of August and Cory left the first of July. But not until after he and Marc had had yet another loud, extended argument about accounts. Cory had stormed out of the office telling Marc that "This isn't over yet."

On July 10th, I got a long email from Cory, telling me about his adventures:

> Cutter—You won't believe it. Got here fine and got settled in. Nolan, Brett and I took a bus at 6:00 in the morning to the city so we could be on the race track by the 7:00 deadline. An American named Cortez saw us on the bus and says to himself, "no way those guys are running, too clean. Then I look down and see Nolan's Superman socks and I say to myself, these guys ARE running." He comes over and introduces himself and starts to tell us the story of his run the day before. He's talking a mile a minute and

the story he tells is a little concerning, and we can't appreciate his words yet, but everything he said was exactly how it went down for us. I'm pretty scared, Nolan is nervous and Brett is feeling okay. In Brett's words, "I'm not too bad, until the first fireworks go off, and I look at Cory, and he has a look on his face that I've never seen on someone's face, and it scares me like never before." At that moment, every plan, goal and idea of this run goes right out the window. Now you only have one plan and one goal. Survive. I've never felt this scared in my entire life. So the course is about 900 yards. Cortez suggests we start after dead man's curve. We agree. This leaves about 500 yards we have to run to the arena. As the bulls come down, they have gates at certain points to close the course off so the bulls can't turn around if one strays from the pack. There is also a gate at the arena, so if you don't keep up with the bulls, the gates close, you don't get in. Getting in is a big deal. Locals around us are getting on their knees to pray, kissing a poster of the Mother Mary and sprinting to warm up. Not something we wanted to see. The first firework sounds to let everyone know it's time. The second firework goes off to let you know the gate is open and the bulls are heading your way. People around us start to jog so we figure that's probably what we should do. Not only are the bulls a problem but people in front of you falling are just as much a concern. So the whole time you're having to check your front then check your back over and over again. I get about 100 yards down and we slow down to almost a stop. For me it was completely silent except for what I needed to hear. All your senses are at their highest. I look down to the curve and all I can see is the people coming. All of a sudden the heads start to move in a pattern and the crowd at the curve starts to scream and yell. The bulls are making the turn but you can't see them. You know they are there, so I take the fuck off down the road faster than I've ever moved. Again looking forward then back over and over. Everything goes quiet and all I can hear is the bells around their necks and the sound is getting louder. People are starting to fall in front of me. I keep looking back and see nothing, nothing, nothing and then they're right next to you. They're massive. Not a lot you can do but pray they don't move too close to you. I have to hurdle two people, Brett stepped on a guy's hand. Once they pass I start to slow down. I can't breathe and I'm ready to give up. I'm not making it to the arena. I look up and see the arena about 50 yards in front of me. I get back on the horse and start running for the hallway to the arena before they close the gates. You get into the area and the crowd is cheering you on. You feel like a gladiator. I almost break down but then they release a bull into the arena to chase around everyone so I'm back in alert mode. I stayed on the side while people antagonized the bull. We run into each other inside and we're all hugging. Hugging random strangers. It was a great feeling. You felt like you had lived through something and that's all you could ask for. It was unbelievable.

I laughed out loud reading his story, picturing Cory dressed in white with a red sash around his waist, running for his life. I kind of envied his adventure but knew I was too chickenshit to ever do something like that myself. So I was really shocked when, two days later, Marc called us altogether to tell us Cory had died.

THIRTEEN

CUTTER

There was an audible gasp from the folks in the room. Cory was kind of the glue which held us all together, the heart of the place. KC, in a decidedly un-Fulton Flash-like display, wept loudly. I assumed Cory had done something stupid, like trying to outrun the bulls one more time. I was wrong. According to Marc, Cory had committed suicide. Everyone, especially me, was stunned. It just didn't sound like Cory, leastwise the Cory Jones we knew. Mary Beth asked, "Are they sure? How do they know it was a suicide? Maybe it's a mistaken identity."

Marc shook his head slowly. "Cory's girlfriend found him. He'd shot himself, the gun was lying next to him. There was a note on his computer."

"What did the note say?" Lowry asked.

"We don't know. The Spanish authorities haven't released any of the details. When they do, they'll be sent to the U.S. Embassy and then on to the family here."

"When did it happen? Wasn't he in Spain to run with the bulls?" Mary Beth wanted to know.

"Apparently two nights ago. Cory had done the bull run thing earlier that day." I heard the sharp intake of air into my own lungs. Marc turned toward me and asked, "What?"

"Nothing," I answered, but my mind was going a thousand miles an hour. That was the night he wrote me. How could he write what he did and then commit suicide? It made no fucking sense. How could I not know something was wrong? Why didn't he say anything? The only experience I had with suicide involved a woman I had loved, but she had killed herself many months after she left my life. According to her family, there were signs, though, of course, they only saw the signs after she was dead. Had we done the same thing with Cory? What could have been so bad, so horrible he chose death over it? Did he do the run-with-the-bulls thing to feel really alive before he died because he was sick? Questions. Lots of questions and no answers, at least not yet. We all made our ways to our own spaces to deal with it in our own manners. Ten minutes later I walked through the office and told folks they could leave if they wished. An hour later, only KC, Marc, Rachel and I remained.

Rachel came into my office shortly before noon and asked if I wanted to go to lunch, and more to the point, if I "wanted to go drink my lunch" with her. I told her okay and asked where she wanted to go. She suggested O'Connell's up on King Street. We walked the dozen blocks or so in silence.

"Good choice," I told her when we entered. "An Irish pub is the perfect place to hold a wake." She looked at me like I was being sarcastic so I assured her I was dead serious. "Really, Rachel, this place is perfect." We snagged a high-backed booth and I ordered a black and tan. Rachel ordered a scotch and soda. I raised my eyebrows.

She defended herself, "Hey, if there was ever a time that required liquor in the middle of the day, this is it."

"That's not it," I told her. "But scotch in an Irish pub? Really? How *gauche*." For the first time all day, Rachel smiled. Which made me smile. I silently marveled at how she could do exactly the right thing at the right time to pick up my spirits, from chocolate chip cookies and gin on a car seat, to bringing me to this place. Our drinks came and we ordered lunch. Bangers and mash for me—my go-to Irish pub order—and she wanted the shepherd's pie. The server left us to talk about the cloud over our heads.

"Cutter, you knew Cory much better than I. What do you think happened?"

"I really don't know. It confounds me. And makes me angry." I felt tears in my eyes. I gathered myself and told her about the email from Cory the night he died. She wanted to hear it. She smiled and nodded her head as I read it to her. She sat quietly after I finished. "So does that sound like someone who is going to off himself?"

She shook her head slowly. "No, it sure doesn't."

We reminisced about Cory throughout lunch, mostly me telling stories of his very unorthodox means of getting clients to sign on the dotted line. Her favorite tale was about the time I was giving the Director of FEMA a tour of our offices and Cory sidled up to me and said, in a perfect imitation of Cousin Eddie from *Christmas Vacation*, "Place sure looks nice, Clark." When I broke out laughing, the Director slowly moved away from us. There were enough funny stories, and drinks, to put us in a better mood, a proper Irish wake. I told her about Cory's recent fights with Marc and her face darkened and she frowned. I asked her what was wrong.

"There is another reason I asked you to lunch today." She paused, ran her fingers through her hair and bit her lower lip. "Almost immediately after Marc told us about Cory, he asked me to come to his office. He was quite cordial, but, I don't know, somehow cold, removed, something. No emotion, no mention of Cory."

"What did he want?"

"He asked if I would be the new Chief Financial Officer."

"Wow!" I was genuinely surprised. And pleased. "That's terrific. I assume you told him 'yes'."

"I did. Also, and I hope you are okay with this, he offered me Cory's share of the company." I scowled before I could catch myself, then forced a smile. Too late. She'd seen my reaction. "Is there something wrong with that?"

I had to admit, "No. Nothing. I had just hoped that someday I would get a small piece of the action. I'm just being petty. But I don't get it. That share belongs to Cory's estate, probably to his parents."

Rachel explained, "The partners all have the right to acquire any other partner's share upon separation from the company. Marc said they will buy my share as a signing bonus."

"Holy shit. That's got to be worth a pretty penny. Well done, Ms. Red Cloud, well done." I grinned and meant it. She took my hands and squeezed them tightly.

"So I should do it?" she asked.

"Hell yes, you should do it. There are a couple of things you need to know about," and I told her two stories. The first was about what had happened with Marc's family and his tendency to show signs of PTSD.

When I finished, she said quietly, more to herself than to me, "Maybe that's why he acted the way he did about Cory." Then to me, "What else?" I told her about Marc and Cory fighting over Marc's use of some company accounts. She surprised me with her response.

"Oh, I know about that. I was the one who discovered it and told Cory. I brought it up to Marc when he offered me the position. He told me he would be using only one account which would not have my name on it, so I'm okay with handling it that way."

"Should we be worried about it?"

"No, I think it is okay if he does it that way."

I congratulated her again, we finished our drinks and made our way back to the office just in time to leave for the day. I thanked Rachel for taking such good care of me. She hugged me tightly and told me it was all her pleasure. She couldn't have been more wrong. The pleasure was indeed all mine.

Everyone from AMASS attended the memorial service for Cory and after the initial outpouring of Cory stories, we pretty much bore our grief silently and alone. We were in the dog days of D.C. heat and humidity and the preparation for the end of fiscal year buying spree. We were dismayed, though not surprised, to see a sharp drop in spending. The economy was doing well, very well, but the federal government was in shambles.

After the new Prez's hordes of government novices invaded the White House, all semblance of order disappeared. Within the first six months he hired and fired willy-nilly and nothing of any real value was accomplished. He maintained a good relationship with the speaker of the house, who like him, was a closet bigot, but fought almost daily with the majority leader in the Senate. No legislation could get passed, even though the Republicans held control of both houses as well as the presidency. Cabinet appointments moved so slowly the departments' work ground to a standstill. It was the worst gridlock anyone could remember.

Just like the carpenter who only has a hammer and thus treats everything like a nail, the Prez returned to what worked for him. He held rallies of his (dwindling but still rabid) followers where he felt safe and appreciated. Nero fiddling. Meanwhile rumors started circulating the Russians had somehow manufactured Connard's election, up to and including tampering with ballots. There were no bullets yet, but plenty of smoking guns. We sat on the sidelines and said to any Republican who would listen, "Told you so."

Finally, in September, the Spanish government released the reports regarding Cory's suicide. He had had a lot to drink after his run with the bulls, not surprisingly, but no drugs. He had apparently eaten a large meal late in the evening, as is the Spanish custom. None of his friends or his family, not even his girlfriend, thought anything was wrong or out of the ordinary. His friends said he had been planning this adventure for several years. He had no diseases and in fact was in great health, knocking my theory out of contention. The note he left said he had been manipulating AMASS accounts to cover gambling debts, but no one would verify those claims and Marc declined to have the books examined

113

or to press charges. His partners agreed. The only other unanswered question was how he obtained, in Spain, the Glock G28 handgun with which he killed himself. Even more puzzling was the fact the Glock G28 is made special for and only sold to law enforcement agencies. The authorities could not determine the gun's origins.

Sandy spent the late summer recess in Iowa with Congresswoman Buday, leaving me in charge of the house. Actually, she left Maria Fuentes, our newly acquired live-in mother, in charge. It was working out pretty well, this having a fifth member of the family who took care of us. She was a better cook than either of us, she was great with the kids (and only spoke Spanish to them, requiring them to learn the language) and she was pleasant company. I got lots more play time with Jordan and Livingston. Rachel and Elena spent time with us as well. I found I liked having a big family, I suppose because that's how I'd grown up.

When Sandy returned after Labor Day, we pretty much jettisoned the unacknowledged pretense of a normal connubial relationship. We continued to share a bedroom and bed, we shared parental duties and family time, we shared conversations about our lives and jobs, we shared the occasional dinner date or social engagement, we even shared some laughs. What we did not share was our bodies or our emotions. As long as I didn't think about it (and I didn't), it all worked just fine.

In October, the CDC contacted us and asked if they could run a test of our system with a simulated epidemic. They wanted to actually ID and tag folks, but because it was a test, they wished not to pay for it. Since we had originally agreed to give them the service for free, Marc granted their request. The test went horribly amok, even shut down our system for twelve hours, much to the chagrin of hundreds of career bureaucrats elsewhere in the government. The way Mary Beth explained it to us was the CDC input so many names so quickly from so many different computers, our system simply overloaded. CDC told us in a real emergency they would have to operate in that manner. We increased our capability (at a large cost) twentyfold. Twentyfold was not enough, so we tripled that. The system then seemed to be ready to handle whatever CDC threw at us. We were out half a million dollars, but felt comfortable with the expense. Only because our new CFO told us to feel comfortable.

Two days after we finally passed the CDC test, Julie Barney phoned to tell us she was resigning and accepting a job with CDC. She also confided to me she was living with Dr. Gerstner, but I wasn't to tell her old man. I wasn't surprised and I agreed. It did remind me I hadn't talked to the old fart in quite a while, so I called J. Woodburn for beers and took Rachel along to meet him. I thought he might get a kick out of her. I was right. He made a fool of himself flirting with her all evening. What was worse, she flirted back. I told him a bunch of Cory stories, and, of course, he wanted to use them in a book. I was tempted to tell him about Julie just to throw him off the track. We wished each other happy holidays and promised to get back together after the new year began.

FOURTEEN

MOTHER

The bus driver first poked the man in the shoulder and when he got no response, he shook the guy until his eyes opened. "Hey, *senõr*, this is the end of the line. You need to get off the bus. Get your ass out of that seat."

The man, Juan Suarez, pushed his eyes open, rubbed them and felt the ache which permeated his body. He felt both hot and cold at the same time and shivered under his down parka. He mumbled, "*Dónde estoy?*"

The driver said, "Speak English, Asshole. You're in 'murica now." And then added, "Fuckin' wetbacks." In President Connard's 'murica, such language was not just tolerated, it was encouraged.

Juan worked as a handyman at Villa Amor, a small boutique beachfront hotel on the Pacific Ocean in the coastal village of Sayulita, Mexico. As such, he managed to pick up enough English to ask "Where this?" His head throbbed and he felt like he might puke.

"It's the back of an Indian Trails bus, Asshole. At the end of the line, so you have to get off."

"What place?"

"Marquette, Fucking Michigan. Now get off my damn bus!" The driver grabbed Juan by the hood of his parka and yanked violently. He pulled the disoriented man out of the seat which sent Juan into a paroxysm of violent coughing. Blood and spittle flew from Juan's mouth and landed on the driver's cheek. The driver pushed Juan up the aisle and off the bus into the snowstorm which raged around them. The driver wiped his face on his sleeve and cursed the Mexican one more time.

It was December 3rd and an early blizzard was closing down the entire Upper Peninsula city of Marquette. The bus was the last vehicle into the city during what would be a four-day Artic blast. Marquette was used to this kind of weather, though maybe not this early in the season. Still, everyone was hunkered down and life continued as usual in the godforsaken climate of the U.P.. Folks were still out and about as the common enemy of cold and snow brought people together.

Juan stumbled into the bus station and sank into one of the wooden pews lined up along the wall. His mind came more into focus and a look of pure terror crossed his face. He had gone into the fat Russian's room to fix the toilet and had been distracted by the blonde girl removing her bathing suit. It was the last thing he remembered. Now he was freezing and burning up at the same time, in clothes not his, in a place he had never heard of. He had no idea what had happened to him, but he knew he was very sick and needed help. He reached into his pocket and found fifty American dollars and a driver's license with his picture and name on it. He had never had a driver's license in his life.

He rose to his feet and made his way to the clerk who was just closing her ticket window. "*Por favor*, Ma'am. *Medico*." When he got no response he tried again. "Doctor." He went into another fit of coughing, but covered his mouth to avoid spraying the woman. His eyes rolled up into the back of his head and he collapsed onto the floor like a hundred-pound sack of cornmeal. The clerk gasped and rushed around the counter, pulling her cell phone from her pocket. She hit 911 and then rolled Juan over. Blood seeped from his mouth, nose and eyes. His breathing was labored.

The ambulance arrived twenty minutes later and Juan was carted off to Marquette General Hospital next to the campus of Northern Michigan University. The doctors at Marquette General had never seen symptoms like Juan's and the battery of tests revealed nothing and the treatments they tried had no effect. Two days later Juan Suarez was dead, his body sent to the morgue for autopsy. Within the three days following his death, a bus driver and a clerk from Indian Trails bus line showed up at the hospital with the same symptoms, followed by a paramedic and several hospital staffers. Within days of that, the bus driver's entire family and about forty more people showed up, all showing signs of the disease, yet unidentified by the hospital doctors. By the time a dozen of them had died, and no one was getting better, the doctors sent out a distress call to the Center for Disease Control.

Within twelve hours, Dr. Larry Gerstner and his team of epidemiologists were on the frozen ground of Marquette. Four hours after arriving, one of the CDC doctors had identified the disease as a faster developing strain of Marburg, a close and virulent relative to Ebola, one as yet not encountered. They traced the disease to patient zero, Juan Suarez. They contacted FEMA which arrived later that night. FEMA immediately put the whole city into quarantine. The doctors also contacted authorities in

Sayulita who, it turned out, had been searching for a missing resident named Juan Suarez. Juan had disappeared from work without a trace on November 30th but by all accounts in perfect health when he disappeared. Authorities there also said they had had no outbreak of any disease in Sayulita worse than a hangover.

Investigators for the CDC hunted down the other eight passengers from the bus. Four had already died from the disease. None had encountered any disease where they had been previously. Juan was in fact patient zero. He had been missing for four days. It was as if he had magically disappeared from the hotel in Sayulita and reappeared in the back seat of an Indian Trails bus.

By the middle of January, 16,000 people had died, three fourths of the population of Marquette. The city was devastated. People from all over the country sent aid, though they were almost in a panic the disease might spread to their communities. Supplies of face masks disappeared overnight and the country started to look like a masquerade ball. Thanks to the quarantine instituted by FEMA, the outbreak was contained. However, the CDC required every surviving resident to wear a bracelet which could track them over the following months to insure they were not an unaffected carrier of the disease they now referred to as KM1, Killer Marburg One.

In Washington, the Federal Government was universally lauded for its handling of the disaster, accolades falling on both the CDC and FEMA. Both houses of Congress called for investigations and hearings, yet another way to waste money, and the president started screaming for closing the borders to anyone from Mexico, claiming

"Those people are all infected with this terrible disease and could kill all real Americans." But by April, the Iranians and the president got involved in a major sword rattling confrontation and KM1 and Marquette became yesterday's news. Marquette was left to mourn its dead and try to rebuild its community.

In mid-May, two children, a boy seven years old and a girl five, were found on a train at the Amtrak station in Truckee California. The boy only spoke Arabic and, after an interpreter was located, he explained the girl was his sister and a man in a suit had taken them from their parents and taken them on the train. They had been on the train for two days and the man had been nice to them though the food he gave them tasted bad. He did not know the man's name, but he was an American and he wore glasses and was very tall. He did not know where his parents were. They were from Aleppo and had come to this country to escape the war in Syria.

The girl whispered to her brother and the boy told the interpreter his sister felt ill. The interrupter felt the girl's forehead and immediately called for a doctor. She was burning up with a fever. By the time the doctor finished examining the little girl, the boy complained of aches and pains and they were both taken to the hospital. The country had been on high alert and it took no time to diagnose the children with KM1. The hospital immediately quarantined them and FEMA was on the scene quickly, almost as if they had known the disease was going to show up in Truckee.

FEMA and the CDC quickly chased down the other passengers on the train, isolated the half dozen who had had contact with the children and did blood tests to clear the others. The infection was limited to a couple of the passengers and several of those who had interviewed the boy and girl. All told, only 24 people died, including the two Syrian children, and the town was shut down for a mere three weeks. The tall man with glasses was never located.

While the impact on Truckee was minimal, the impact on the rest of the country was immense. People went from concern to panic. They stayed away from public places and, almost overnight, the retail economy went into a nose dive. Restaurants, cinemas, malls, public transportation and the like all shuttered their doors. The stock market took a massive tumble. The president demanded all borders be closed to everyone, since both cases had come from "vile outsiders." If an unfamiliar person showed up in a small town, he was quickly shown the door. It was just like the Wild West: "We don't much cotton to strangers here, pahdner. Best you keep on movin'."

In early July, coincidentally on the first anniversary of Cory Jones' death, President Connard held a press conference to announce, in his words, "The biggest and best news ever." The Center for Disease Control had developed a vaccine for KM1. He spent several minutes telling the assembled press how he had personally directed the work to develop the medicine, and "Our discovery is more important than those of Louis Pasteur and Jonas Salk." When the press asked him about how the development occurred, he hemmed and hawed for a few minutes and then introduced Dr. Larry Gerstner of the CDC.

"Dr. Gerstner, how were you able to develop the vaccine so quickly, and, as a follow up, has enough been produced for the whole country?" asked the reporter from the *New York Times*. Before Dr. Gerstner could reply, the reporter added, in a surprisingly unreporter-like display, "And congratulations to you and your team. Some fantastic work these last few months." The cameras recorded the look of pure jealousy the president shot at Gerstner.

Larry Gerstner smiled and responded, "Thank you. We have been extremely fortunate to have a great team to work with and President Connard provided all the resources we asked for." Larry Gerstner was sharp enough to know he had to give the Prez kudos, even though the Prez did nothing to deserve them. He continued, "We also were fortunate enough to have a good working relationship with our colleagues at the State Research Center of Virology and Biotechnology Vector, also known as the Vector Institute, in Russia who had already done a yeoman's job on a vaccine for the original strain of Marburg.

"The Russians had an outbreak of Marburg four years ago in Volgograd and several hundred people died. The Institute started working on the immunizer then. They shared their work with us and we were able to make modifications which could block this mutated form of the disease." He paused for questions, but there were none, so he continued. "The vaccine is being produced currently and we should be able to start the immunization process within the next six weeks. We'll begin in the larger cities where people live in close proximity, like New York, and then move on to large cities with less density, like Los Angeles. We will follow that with the rural areas of the country, those areas less susceptible to disease transmission."

Now dozens of hands shot up. Dr. Gerstner smiled again. He knew he was becoming the darling of the press and he was enjoying every minute of it. He recognized each reporter in turn and used the most technical information he could to answer their questions. His ploy worked. They soon quit asking. The president stood once again, took credit for all the work done and exited the stage without acknowledging any of the reporters' waving hands. Larry Gerstner asked for any last questions. There were none. He nodded at his two companions in the back of the room, Julie Barney and Brandon Jones, and left the podium.

Julie beamed. Her man was the hero of the hour. She loved him so much, and while she didn't agree with everything he was doing, she could not say "no" to anything he asked of her. Brandon only nodded in return. But he was very pleased with the way things were going. Mother will be very happy. What made Mother happy, made him happy, or at least what passed for happiness in his somewhat skewed emotional structure. He thought back to how they had gotten here in such a short time and except for the little bump with the kid who worked for Marc Payton, everything was on plan and ahead of schedule. Yeah, Mother will be happy.

One year earlier, Cory Jones had sent a message to Brandon that Marc needed to see him as soon as possible. He met Marc at their assigned safe meeting place. They sat on the bench in Founders Park, facing the Potomac River. The weather was D.C. hot and muggy and thunderheads threatened from the west. Brandon started, "So what is so vital it couldn't wait until our regular meeting?"

"I have a problem I need you to resolve. Cory came to me two days ago and told me he thinks the source of the money coming into my account is Russia and if I don't do something about it, he's going to talk to the IRS and the FBI."

"How did he find the origin of the funding?" Brandon scowled.

"I have no fucking clue, but he has to be dealt with."

"So what do you want me to do? It's not my problem. It's your ass on the line."

Marc took a handkerchief from his pocket and wiped his face. He kept the cloth over his face with both hands and talked into it. "Damnit, Brandon. Just fix it. He's in Spain for two weeks. He can't come back."

"Does Mother know?"

Marc tensed and spat out words, "No! And she isn't to know. Do you understand?"

Brandon Jones smiled, though his smile was more disturbing than comforting. Had he been in an old time movie, he would have twisted the end of his moustache and laughed "Nah-ha-ha." When Brandon was eight years old, he got into a playground fight with a smaller kid, in fact, picked the fight with the boy. After he got the boy down, Brandon sat on his chest and repeatedly punched him in the face, breaking off a couple of teeth and breaking his nose. There was lots of blood and it made Brandon feel good. Powerful. Strong. He wanted more of that feeling. As soon as he could, he found another victim, one he bloodied and concussed.

When it was obvious they had a problem on their hands, Brandon's parents shipped him off to the Georgia Military

Academy. Brandon thrived. He loved the order, he loved the brutality, he loved being applauded for violence. He was both high school boxing champ and karate champ. He soared academically. He was extremely good looking with a physique to match. When it was time to go to college, he chose The Citadel because, as he explained it, West Point was "for pussies." At The Citadel, they taught him how to hurt, maim and kill. And how to plan to do it. And all the rationalization he would ever need to hurt other human beings without guilt. It was the perfect education.

From there, he accepted a commission in the army and in no time found himself in the Rangers. When war broke out, as it did under every Republican president, he was shipped to a Central American country where he could ply his trade in pain. He did so happily. While he was there, destroying bodies and lives with a smile on his face, he learned he could be doing the same thing for a private security company and be much better paid to do the same thing. Without all the stupid rules. As soon as his enlistment was up, he became a mercenary (they referred to themselves as "contractors"), available to the highest bidder. He found himself back in Central America, unfettered by regulations and paid a ridiculous sum. Brandon Jones was in pig heaven.

When he single-handedly slaughtered all of the men in a small village on the flimsiest of excuses, he was quietly released by the company. He was drinking in the Iguana Bar in San Juan del Sur, Nicaragua when he was approached by a tall black woman who introduced herself as "Mother." He was soon on her payroll. He never asked her affiliation because, frankly, he didn't care who employed him, as long as he got to work his art. He was sent to tradecraft school and taught the ways of spydom, though his role was to be an enforcer. He loved his work.

So when Marc asked him to take care of the Cory problem he was quite happy, though he wasn't stupid enough to withhold the information from Mother. Planning the assassination was fun work, figuring out how to do it and when and using what methods. But the killing, the putting the bullet in his head and watching the blood and brains spew out the other side, that was almost orgasmic. He had Cory type on the laptop before he killed him, just to make sure his fingerprints were there so Brandon could write the suicide note afterwards with rubber gloves and have no other prints on the computer.

The only slip-up was forgetting the suicide pistol, so he had to use his own. He hated losing the Glock G28, but he would find a new one to replace it. Damn, that was one fine weapon. He knew it wasn't traceable and figured the inept Spaniards wouldn't know shit from Shinola when it came to handguns. He was, in fact, wrong.

Mother called Brandon two months later to tell him the operation was a go and instructed him to make arrangements with CDC, FEMA and AMASS. The first step was to test the AMASS system in its CDC application. The test failed miserably and Brandon had to strongly remind Marc of his expendability if the system could not be fixed. When Marc complained how much money it would take, Brandon reminded Marc again, this time with gun in hand. Half a million of Marc's dollars later, the system worked.

He flew down to Atlanta to brief Dr. Larry Gerstner. Gerstner and his team chose a location, one which would be isolated enough the chances of a wide-spread epidemic starting were low, especially since they would wait until the correct weather was forecast. When the weather service alerted them to the early blizzard heading to the Upper Peninsula of Michigan, the plan went live. Gerstner provided the vial of virus to FEMA, Mother's agent in Mexico provided patient zero, also to FEMA, and five days later Marquette, Michigan was the site of the worst disease epidemic in America since the Spanish flu. The CDC and FEMA had tagged every single person left alive with AMASS's system and could now track their every move. Those potential victims had been warned if they removed the plastic bracelets it would lead to their arrest. Everyone obeyed the law.

Five months later, the team repeated its performance in Truckee, California. The ensuing national panic worked to perfection. After Gerstner announced the creation of the vaccine, he and Brandon stood in the CDC warehouse and admired the huge stacks of cases of the Russian-manufactured medicine. They both smiled. At the same time, Mother stood at the window of her penthouse in the Connard Hotel in Manhattan, nodded her headed and also smiled.

FIFTEEN

CUTTER

Like the rest of America, we watched in horror as a small town in Michigan, one most of us had never heard of, was devastated by the outbreak of a new killer virus. Unlike the rest of America, AMASS was actually able to help do something about it. The CDC was going to use our system to track any potential spread of the disease. Fortunately for us, Julie Barney had insisted just a couple of months before we test the system. And luckily, that test led to the changes which insured we operated flawlessly when the time came. After receiving probably worthless guarantees of our safety, Mary Beth and I flew to Marquette to serve as liaisons with the CDC.

I had not been in weather as cold and snowy since I left the Rockies. Luckily I still had the clothes for it. Mary Beth, on the other hand, had shown up at the airport in a leather jacket and some thin leather gloves and no hat. We actually had to make our first stop at an outdoor store, one which FEMA opened just for us. We were bivouacked at a chain hotel on the outskirts of the city and issued face masks and hazmat suits to wear any time we left the building. I chose not to, not that I was afraid or anything, but... Well, fuck, I was scared to death. I'd never been this close to a real life disaster ever. Mary Beth, on the other hand, had to go to the intake center where they were registering folks and tagging them. She was scared, but she bucked up like a real trooper and did her job. I asked Rachel if we could give her hazard pay and Rachel doubled her salary for the time we were there. She didn't double mine.

Once we were on the ground in Marquette, we were quarantined like the rest of the city, so I missed all of the holidays with my family. We were not released until the end of January. I was tired of being cold, I was tired of being cooped up, I was tired of being bored. After I returned to D.C., I spent three straight days with Jordan and Livingston, doing nothing but playing while Maria took care of us. Sandy even took an afternoon off to play. My first day back at work, I walked into an office which was decorated for a party, a party for Mary Beth and me. Turned out, AMASS had made over two million dollars for its efforts during the disaster. We were feted for our contribution to everyone's fiscal well-being. As long as I didn't think about the 16,000 who had had to die for us to make money, I was happy. Still.

Things settled down in our office, just as they did in D.C.. Over the year Connard and his cronies were in the White House, the strength of the bureaucracy exerted itself and the government's work plodded on. The country remained divided over the issue of Harry Connard. Folks fell into one of three categories, those who supported him and still loved him, those who had supported him but now felt buyer's regret and those who had opposed him. The "fors" continually turned a blind eye to the Prez's screw-ups and when cornered, would point to the screw-up of some other politician, maybe from years before. They were still in love with The Connard. The "againsts" were just as vocal as they had been, if not more so, and were happy the mainstream press was on their side. Those who suffered from buyer's regret quietly tucked their tails between their legs and skulked off to hide.

In early May, Rachel asked me to dinner. We left the office about four and she drove. She took 495 into Maryland, exited on Route 4 and made her way down to Chesapeake Beach to the Rod 'N' Reel restaurant, a trip which took an hour or so. When I asked why we were going so far, she told me to wait. We got to the waterfront restaurant, ordered drinks and I asked her, "Okay, what gives? Why are we out here in the middle of nowhere?"

Rachel thought for a few seconds, then asked me, "Cutter, do you know what forensic accounting is?"

"No, not really."

"Basically, it is a specialized area of accounting which is used by the courts, or those going to court. It covers everything from fraud to money laundering. It's the same basic principles as regular accounting, but is even more exact."

"Okay, and?" I asked.

"Back in Colorado, I did accounting work for the tribal council, *pro bono*. Because the council was under federal law and their finances were under constant scrutiny, I took forensic courses to be able to represent them in court if necessary."

I wasn't sure where she was going with this, but I was entertained by the cloak and dagger approach she had taken, so I urged her on, "And you're telling me this why?"

"I spent several months going over the books trying to find where Cory had screwed with them. I did it when no one else was in the office, nights and weekends." She paused, maybe for effect. "Cutter, Cory never used any AMASS account to support a gambling, or any other, habit. The accounts are as clean as a whistle, except for the money from the numbered accounts Marc moved around. And even that doesn't seem to be illegal, just sketchy, because we don't know the origin. It was just money in, money out. We didn't launder it, because we would have had to show it as income, and we never did. Understand?"

"I understand what you are saying, but I'm not sure I see your point."

"I don't think Cory killed himself. Between the suicide note not standing up to my research, and the last email he sent you, it feels wrong. That's why we came all the way out here. So we wouldn't be overheard by anyone. I'm not given to paranoia, but I think this is all very strange."

I thought about what she had said. Cory's death never did seem to fit. I asked her, "So what do we do?"

"I don't know. I thought you might have some idea."

"Let me think about it. But let's not share this with anyone."

"Agreed."

We finished our meal, talked about mundane things and drove back to Alexandria. Over the next few days I thought a great deal about what Rachel had said. I pulled out not only the last email Cory had sent me, but all of our correspondence from the previous six months or so. Nowhere could I find any clue to what was wrong. He had told me if he couldn't get the accounts straightened out, I should be worried, but he never told me why. Nor did he tell me if he had gotten them fixed.

Just as I needed a distraction from that conundrum, word came in from Truckee, California about another outbreak of KM1. As expected, we got the call to come assist. Mary Beth quickly volunteered, I suspect because she liked the double salary and because like all young people she felt invincible. I felt I did not want to tempt fate twice, so I asked KC to go. I felt a little bad about putting her in harm's way. But just a little. Rachel paid her double salary for the time as well, which assuaged my guilt a little. But just a little.

The outbreak was quickly contained, our folks weren't quarantined, and the CDC ended up only tagging about 500 people, so we made very little money this time. The country was in a panic, people calling for the banning of all immigrants, in fact, some wanted to shut the borders entirely. The president threatened to declare a state of emergency and enact martial law. When the Supreme Court blocked him from doing it, President Connard held a series of rallies where he preached a litany of nationalism and called for the closure of the "kangaroo courts". Only the widespread fear of KM1 kept the crowds from becoming too large and turning into lynch mobs. For once, the Democrats had used social media to fight Connard; every time a rally was announced the Dems would bombard the internet with warnings and rumors about the danger of contracting KM1 in crowds. There was no scientific proof of that claim, but it worked fine with Connard's supporters—they didn't believe in scientific proof anyway.

Before the entire nation could erupt in a second civil war, President Harry Connard held a press conference to announce the development of a vaccine for KM1 which would be made available very soon, and more surprisingly, at no cost to the public. How terribly unRepublican. We watched the press conference and saw our old friend Dr. Larry Gerstner on stage with the Prez. I even saw Julie in a pan shot of the audience and called old man Barney to let him know his baby girl was on TV. All of us at AMASS were excited to be a part of this little piece of history and to have our very own Julie Barney right there in the thick of it. No one seemed more excited than Marc. He went around the room congratulating everyone (though we had absolutely nothing to do with the vaccine) and slapping people on the back. Marc had been in one of his lows after news of Cory reached us and for the first time since, he seemed to be relaxed and happy.

In August, Maria took several weeks off to visit her family in whatever Central American village she was from. The name of the village escapes me, but I remember it has a lot of Xs and Ps in it. The kids could tell you. Their Spanish was becoming quite passable and I was happy they were learning a second language. I never had and always felt guilty about it, me, the ugly American. I took Portuguese at Northwestern and retained only two words, *dia bom*. If I was ever introduced to a person from Brazil or Portugal, I could tell them "good day." So far, it hadn't happened. I figured the kids would be very happy to have Maria gone for a while and get their parents back to parenting. And not have to speak only Spanish to get something to eat. I was wrong. Within two days all Sandy and I heard was, "When is Maria coming back?" And Livingston made the mistake of telling his mother, "Why can't you cook good like Maria?" We all got cereal for dinner that night.

For a change though, Sandy and I were spending a lot more time together with the forced parenting chores. I had told her, of course, about Cory dying, but nothing else of the circumstances surrounding the suicide. I shared what Rachel had told me. Her response was totally unexpected.

"Cutter, I understand if you can't tell me, but you guys have done work with the CDC and FEMA, right?"

"Yep, but nothing we have done there has required SECRET status. Why?"

"Well this does, understand?" I nodded my head in agreement. She went on, "There is a discussion going on in military intelligence circles about KM1 and its origin. There is a theory the virus is not naturally occurring, that it was purposefully mutated to be used as a biological weapon."

"How did it get released?" I wanted to know.

"Keep in mind, it's only a theory. I just wondered if the CDC might be thinking the same thing."

"I haven't heard a thing, but if you want I'll ask Julie to keep her ears open."

"No. Leave it alone, but let me know if you hear anything about it, okay?"

I agreed, but asked her, "Why did Cory's suicide make you ask that question?"

"Cutter, you know the congresswoman is on the military intelligence subcommittee. Well, working with those guys makes a person paranoid. They see nefarious motives behind everything that happens. They think everything bad is connected to everything else bad. I deal with one junior officer who is convinced the president is a Russian spy, even though everyone tells him the president isn't smart enough to know a secret code from a haiku." I laughed and she went on, "Anyway, when two bad things happen and there is a nexus, all this spy talk makes a person wonder."

"I'll keep my ears open, but I sure see no connection. We're not exactly spy central, you know." I paused, then decided I had to broach the subject. "Can I ask you a question?"

"You may," she answered, correcting my grammar.

"This young man of yours, is it serious?"

She sat quietly, her face an absolute mask of stillness. Finally, she smiled, but there was a kind of sadness in her eyes. She spoke softly, "I think it is. I don't want to hurt you, again, but Stephen is very important to me."

"Stephen?"

"Stephen Scott. I don't want to give up our family, but I don't want to lose him either. He has been pushing me to leave and I can't. I can't desert the kids and the family. I don't know what to do." Her voice trailed off and I was shocked to see tears roll down her cheeks. I did what I always do when a woman cries, I put my arm around her shoulder. I felt sorrow for her. I didn't, and still don't, want her to be unhappy or suffer. There was a time I did, but that time was gone. I stroked her hair and told her everything would work out for the best. I'm not sure what I meant, but I was serious. She cried for a while, got up and hugged and thanked me. I felt a calm I had not felt in years.

The next day at lunch I told Rachel about the conversation with Sandy. She was moderately interested in the information about KM1. She was very interested in the information about Stephen Scott. "Cutter, we've known each other for several years and I consider you one of my dearest friends. Is there some reason you never tell me about stuff in your personal life?" She sounded a bit piqued.

"I don't know. Guess I feel like I should keep my problems to myself. Why bother you with them?"

"Maybe because I'm your friend." Then she asked, "What does all that mean to your and Sandy's marriage?"

"I don't know that either. I want my kids to have a happy childhood, like I had. To me, everything else is secondary. Except the job. That's way below secondary."

After we finished eating, we walked back in silence. I opened the door to the office for her and, as she walked through it, she put her hand on my arm and squeezed. She whispered, "I won't wait forever," and walked on into the building. I stood there with my mouth open. Christ in a hand basket.

SIXTEEN

CUTTER

I had had a crush on Rachel Red Cloud from the day I met her. It wasn't just about her beauty, though that was undeniable. She had a quiet intensity oddly paired with softness. She always seemed so serious, though she was frequently the first to laugh at clever *bon mots*. I had seen her drink, but never drunk. I had seen her laugh, but never giggle. I had seen her fierce, but never mean. I had seen her reserved, but never disingenuous. Everything about her was attractive, though she never appeared to welcome attention.

Rachel Red Cloud had been born Chu'Manam, meaning "Snake Maiden," into the Hopi tribe and married into the Dakota tribe. She had taken the name Rachel when she left her home in the Four Corners to attend the University of Colorado in Boulder. There she had met Billy Red Cloud, who was, in fact, a minor chieftain in the Dakota tribe. Billy was a wild man, exceptionally good looking and considered a very good catch. Rachel had never met anyone like him. She was shy and studious, given to spending most of her time alone in the library. Billy forced her out of that hermit-like life. She still managed to graduate *summa cum laude,* but before she graduated, she was married and had a baby.

After college, Billy had moved them to Columbus, Colorado to pursue one get-rich scheme after another. Rachel had been happy to be a stay-at-home mom, doing part-time jobs like tax accounting and bookkeeping for a couple of small businesses. When Billy, who by now wanted to be called The Chief, lost the remainder of his meager inheritance in a silver mine attraction for tourists, Rachel had to go to work. She took a civil service test, which she aced, and was hired by the city parks department after her first interview. Within two years, she was the chief financial officer for the department and that's where I met her. While she was not officially my number two, she certainly was unofficially. She saved my butt more than once, and soon became one of my best friends. I have to admit, I had entertained fantasies about her, but it never got in the way of our friendship. If she had ever shown any interest in me, it was way too subtle for my finely tuned radar. As we've established, subtlety is not my strong suit.

I stood holding the door of the office open long enough for someone to yell I was letting out the AC. I was frozen, not sure how to respond. Or even if I should respond. Over the next few days, I did my best to not act rattled and tried to keep everything on a professional footing. At the end of the third day, after the office had cleared out, I walked into her office and offered her my hand. She stood and I kissed her like I meant it. Because I did. I left without saying anything.

We seemed to immediately come to some unspoken agreement, though I couldn't have put it into words. There was no emotional tension between us. It felt terribly warm and comforting. I smiled a lot and we ate lunch together most every day. I'm sure folks noticed, but frankly I didn't give a shit.

September took Sandy back to Iowa for the month, gearing up for the biennial congressional election. She was happy to be with

Buday's chief political staffer, one Stephen Scott, where it was natural for them to spend a lot of time together. Before she left, she shared with me the latest on the KM1 vaccine and the schedule for getting the populace inoculated. Turned out, all elected officials, their staffs and families were to be the first to be vaccinated. Next on the schedule were all government employees, then all government contractors. After that, inoculation centers would be set up in every major city and the public would be treated. All anyone would need to get the shot was a Social Security number. No name, no address, no other information would be gathered. Easy peasy. The whole family got the shot the day before Sandy left. I was surprised by how relieved I felt seeing the kids get that shot. Safe.

As soon as the announcement was made about the vaccination schedule, the anti-vaccine bloc went on the warpath, asserting such vaccines caused everything from autism to cancer, syphilis to insanity. That it was all a government plot to control the populace. While there are reasonable concerns about some vaccines, though nothing as yet proven scientifically, this group took a broadband approach and attacked anything called a vaccine. Within days, suits were filed all over the country to stop any vaccinations.

The CDC argued the safety of the general population took precedent over the beliefs of a few and everyone should be required to be inoculated. The program went ahead for all government employees and contractors, but several courts issued restraining orders and the process ground to a halt until the cases could make their way up to the Supreme Court.

In late September as centers stood ready, but unused, to administer the medicine, we woke up to screaming news people announcing a new outbreak of KM1. It had swept unchecked through Belle Glade, Florida, where over-worked doctors failed to identify the disease and within four days 15,000 people were infected. The mortality rate was over 90 percent. Patient zero was an immigrant who had just arrived from Cuba. That afternoon the Supreme Court heard arguments, the anti-faction rendered impotent by the day's news. Not only did the Court order mandatory vaccinations, it also authorized the temporary banning of immigrants and held the president could order martial law should additional outbreaks require it.

We were not called to Belle Glade to assist the CDC. They believed their staff was capable of handling the tagging of potential victims, especially since Julie Barney led their team. There were so few people left who were not infected, they used very few slots. Only Mary Beth was disappointed.

The CDC estimated it would take about four months to complete the program. It began slowly but within a few days, photographs of the previous victims dying and dead appeared on the internet. The photos painted a picture of a painful and gruesome death. Dr. Gerstner released a statement apologizing for the photographs being released and promised the firing of whoever had done it. But the following day, every one of the centers had lines out the door by early morning.

I watched the news coverage as I made breakfast for the kids. Maria had graciously allowed me to keep this one parental chore.

This morning was waffles and sausage, Livingston's favorite. Mostly he liked how he got to put syrup on everything. His preschool teacher was not as happy, since he showed up on those days with sticky fingers and a sugar buzz. The morning show had a live feed from the Northern Virginia KM1 intake center. Where chaos reigned.

When I was about twelve years old I got my first job, working on my friend Charlie Miller's family turkey farm. The job was the inoculating of turkeys for a host of poultry diseases they didn't describe, and which I didn't want to know about. There was a huge pen filled with about 5,000 turkeys. Next to it was a pen with no turkeys. The pens were connected by three chutes. My assignment was to pick up a turkey, hold it tightly and carry it into a chute. There my friend Charlie would grab the turkey's waddle and inject it with a syringe attached to a jug of medicine in the backpack he wore. Release the turkey in the empty pen. Repeat 1,000 times, since there were six turkey holders and three inoculators. After ten minutes, I didn't notice the smell, but when I got home, my mom, eyes watering, hustled me out the door and told me I had to sleep outside. Three days and 5,000 turkeys later, my clothes were burned and I was scrubbed in the back yard, but I had more money than I had ever had before. I was correct when I assumed every job after that one would be a step up.

The news broadcasts of the KM1 program looked exactly like that first job. People were herded into single lines, they gave a clerk at a computer their Social Security number, a nurse or doctor plunged a hypodermic needle into their arm and they exited the back door. The only deviation was for those few without a Social Security number. Those few had to fill out the long form with all of their personal information and were assigned a special number until their Social Security number was issued. Everyone was given an official notice of inoculation which was to be presented to any law enforcement official or medical staff who might ask to see it. Failure to comply would mean either a fine or re-inoculation. The shot was just painful enough no one would volunteer to have a second dose. The only side effects reported were headaches and/or problems with hearing, neither of which seemed to be long lasting.

It soon became apparent the process of immunizing America was going to take longer than the four months the CDC originally estimated. By the end of November, six weeks into the program, only ten million people had been immunized, a rate which would mean almost eight months to reach everyone in the country. The president ordered FEMA to also open KM1 centers and by year's end, an additional twenty million had been treated. Still not satisfied with the speed, the president ordered up the National Guard to administer additional sites and by February, forty million Americans per month were getting the injection.

It was about that time, KC, The Fulton Flash, wandered into my office late one afternoon. With the national attention on KM1 and its prevention and with the current administration's attack on those programs which actually benefitted folks other than the rich, not many agencies were buying our program. We still had existing customers and they generated some cash, but no one was adding or changing many employees. KC was still making sales calls, but she was getting squat for her efforts. She looked depressed.

"What's up?" I asked her.

She plopped into a chair and sighed, then started bouncing around in her seat. Even when The Flash was depressed, she was a bundle of energy. She pursed her lips together, brow furrowed. Finally, she told me, "Cutter, I had Mary Beth run some diagnostic tests, just as a routine maintenance exercise. She found something that may be something or not."

"What?"

"You remember how we had the glitch a year ago or so where numbers disappeared?"

"Vaguely," I told her. Cutter-speak for I didn't remember at all.

"Well it's happened again."

"So?"

"It doesn't affect our capabilities at all, but millions of numbers have just disappeared. And not sequential numbers. Completely random. So it's not one agency using them."

"Millions? Sounds pretty damned serious to me. We need to get Norman and his folks to look at it, don't you think?"

"Nah. Mary Beth says it's nothing to worry about. We use a ten-digit number, so the loss means nothing really."

"Well, it sounds serious."

"A ten-digit number means we have ten billion different numbers, enough to assign one to every person on earth and still have enough for a third more. So, no, it's not serious. Unless it increases. I just thought you should know."

"Okay." She didn't move to leave, so I asked, "Are you okay? You seem a little down."

"I don't know. This place just hasn't felt right since Cory…" her voice trailed off.

"I know. You want to take some time off?"

"Nope. I guess I need something exciting to happen," and she finally gave me a small smile.

"I'll figure something out for you," I told her. We chatted for a while and then collected Rachel, Mary Beth and a couple of staff and went for a beer. By the end of the evening, The Fulton Flash was back to her usual self and my concern waned.

You ever had the sensation of waking from a dream feeling an emotion, though you can't remember the dream? Like anger or fear or happiness? About a week after KC had come to see me, I woke up in the middle of the night, knowing I had had a dream I couldn't quite pull up as a memory, but I felt ill at ease, like something was wrong. I lay in bed for a few minutes, alone, since Sandy was back in Iowa doing a series of town hall meetings for the congresswoman. I roused myself enough to get up and check on the children and even on Maria. They were all fine.

I couldn't go back to sleep. Finally, as it was wont to do, my mind drifted to Sandy and our arrangement. Which led me to our conversation where she had used the word "nexus." What had she said about a nexus of bad things happening? There was Cory, there was the odd use of AMASS's accounts, our involvement with the CDC and KM1, and now KC's being concerned about missing numbers. I bounced between those thoughts, but could come up with no meaningful connection, except it all revolved around AMASS. Just as I was drifting back to sleep, it hit me. I got up, made some coffee and opened my computer. I typed up everything I could remember about all those issues, a full five pages of notes. As always, writing helped me sort it out. My profs at Northwestern would have been proud. They always contended writing helped anyone see things more clearly.

At 7:00 in the morning, 6:00 her time, I called Sandy. She was awake. "Hey, it's me. Gotta second?"

"Yes. What? Are the kids okay?"

"They're great," then thought she might take that wrong and added, "but they miss you. I have a request. Can you get me in to see Congresswoman Buday when you guys get back?"

"Depends. What's it concerning?"

"Remember our 'nexus' conversation? It's about that."

"Am I included?"

"If you wish. But no one else. Got it?"

She paused and then told me, "All right. We'll be back next week. I'll set it up."

"Thanks. See you then."

She didn't sign off. "Cutter, is everything okay? You sound worried."

"Not worried, just want not to feel guilty for not sharing something. In case it means anything."

"Okay. Talk to you later." We hung up.

SEVENTEEN

MOTHER

At 1:00 a.m. on Thanksgiving morning, President Connard padded down the stairs leading from the residence in the White House, his bald head shiny with perspiration. He made his way to the desk of the Secret Service officer on duty. The officer looked up and smiled. He knew what a late night visit meant.

"Shall I call Marine One?" the officer asked, referring to the presidential helicopter.

"Yes. Pronto. I'll be out in ten minutes." Connard turned on his heel and hurried into a downstairs dressing room where he changed into black slacks and a too tight black turtleneck sweater. He thought the outfit made him look svelte and menacing. It made the secret service agents think he looked like a huge bowling ball, but they did their best not to smile. As promised he strode out to the helipad ten minutes later. Marine One was already waiting for him.

"The usual, sir?" the marine guard asked. Connard nodded his head. This is not how he wanted to start his Thanksgiving. He wanted to fly down to Florida for a few days of feasting and golf.

Ninety minutes later, the helicopter landed on the pad atop the Connard Hotel in Manhattan. The agents accompanying the president knew exactly what to do. They escorted him into the elevator which went one floor down to the penthouse. There they remained outside the suite's door. This was not the first time a president had entertained a special lady friend on the side and the Secret Service always handled their job discreetly. The only difference with this one was no one had been able to find out much about the older black woman he met there.

They knew her name, they knew she spent her first ten years in North Carolina, they knew her parents were both college professors who died in a traffic accident when they were visiting professors in Vienna and that she was fostered by an Austrian professor and her husband until she finished college at age 22. They knew she had worked for Connard Resorts for many years. They did not know how she had become Connard's mistress. Connard did not visit often and his visits did not last long, generally three hours or less. But she must have been very good. The president always came out looking flushed and relaxed.

Connard punched the code into the security lock and let himself in. He walked slowly down the hall to the large and under-furnished living room. Mother sat in a high-backed chair overlooking the city skyline. She did not turn around or acknowledge him when he arrived. He cleared his throat and asked in the quietest voice he could muster, "You needed to see me?"

"We have a problem." The response gave Connard a chill. No one wanted to have a problem with Mother.

"Yes, ma'am. What can I do to help?" No one would have recognized this acquiescent Harry Connard. There was exactly zero of the trademark bluster in his voice.

Mother said even more quietly, "The program is going way too slowly and Moscow is not happy. You need to step it up and step it up now."

"We're doing everything we can. Gerstner has all his folks in the field. It's just going to take longer."

"Not a good enough answer, Harry. Use FEMA, call out the National Guard, use the army. You're the president. Act like it." This she said much louder.

"Yes, ma'am," was his entire response. As always, when their business was completed, Connard retired to a small office off the main hallway. There he waited until enough time had passed to continue the charade of a torrid love affair. Two hours later he flew back to the White House, just in time for breakfast with his wife. As always, she did not mention his nighttime disappearing act. The only time she had asked him about it, he had slapped her and told her never to mention it again, to him or anyone else. She had obeyed.

Instead of spending the weekend in Florida, President Connard called a press conference to tell the country he was forgoing his planned Thanksgiving with his family to insure the KM1 immunization would reach more people more quickly. The press lauded his efforts and he was more than eager to take the bows for his statesman-like handling of the crisis facing the country. He called Dr. Gerstner and screamed at him to open more centers, to use FEMA if he needed it.

Larry Gerstner contacted Mother and she told him to go along with the president's orders. He expressed concern with too many people being involved and the risk of discovery being too high. "You know, all we need is for someone to get a sample of the vaccine and do an analysis of it. It wouldn't take much for a lab to

148

see the serum is inert and, even worse, what else is in those injections."

"Lawrence. Let me handle this," Mother almost purred. "We have reached a point where we must take some risks. Harry, I fear, has started to believe the fiction we created for him. His biggest weakness is his ego. True, it is how we managed to forge our relationship with him, but now he believes he is really loved and adored. The number of followers falling into that category is dwindling every day and only those with the saddest lives or greatest hate remain in support. As a result, he says or does the most outrageous things to keep the spotlight on himself. It would only take one major gaffe to bring it all down on his, and our, heads. We have to get this mass vaccination done if we are to succeed. Do you understand?"

"Yes, Mother. I'm on it." He paused, then added, "I hope you heard the first tests were 98 percent accurate. Some we weren't able to track because they were in some kind of shielded area but they showed up on a second or third try. We have found a few whose bodies somehow have rejected the serum. We're working on what may cause that."

"Very good. Keep me apprised. Moscow is quite pleased thus far. I do have one concern at your end."

"Yes?" the doctor asked.

"Your young lady, the Barney girl. Brandon worries she is too close to your efforts and might be a problem, one that he would have to deal with."

"No, no, no. She's fine. You don't have to worry. I have her under control. Tell Brandon to mind his own fucking business,"

Gerstner spat out, then calmed, "Sorry about the language. I apologize. But you can assure everyone Julie is not and will not be a problem."

"All right. Let's get this finished." She hung up before Dr. Gerstner could respond. Mother made a mental note to look more closely into this Julie Barney situation. Her concern came not from what Brandon had said, but from Gerstner's too violent reaction to the accusation. Mother had learned long ago "not a problem" was almost always a problem. Her success came not from her sometimes brilliant operational plans, but from her almost infallible sense of what might go wrong with an operation. She had been trained to look for the downside, and no one had better internalized such training.

Mother was the daughter of an African Russian physicist and a woman who claimed to be descended from the czars. When Mother was five years old her parents were "re-assigned" to work outside of Moscow, and Mother, whose given name was Svetlana, was sent to what was referred to in clandestine circles as "The Charm School", a tongue-in-cheek reference to the Nelson DeMille book of the same name. It was in fact an indoctrination center for the children of dissidents and other enemies of the state. Instructors quickly realized they had been given a brilliant mind in a fierce package and Svetlana was singled out to receive special training to become an agent for the state. By the time she was twenty, she had become a favorite of the head of the KGB, the very same man who devised the strategy to rid Russia of all the resource-draining satellite countries and who later became the president of Russia. By the time she was 22, she was given the identity of a young woman fostered by an Austrian agent. That young woman was buried.

Mother's specific training prepared her to challenge the United States, one of Russia's two primary enemies, the other being China. Her handlers believed her skin color would make her particularly effective working with the Americans. She would always be underestimated by the innate white bigotry of that country. Her handlers were correct. Her first long term assignment was to recruit and train new agents to establish a network of spies to direct in whatever efforts might benefit the homeland. That assignment took her wherever a likely candidate might appear.

For a long time Russia had sought to infiltrate the real power of the United States—corporate America. When Harry Connard unknowingly approached a "lending institution" which was actually a front for the Russian mafia, they saw their opportunity. The Russian mafia owed no allegiance to anyone, save the director of the KGB, because, in fact, that organization of hoods, thieves, killers and mobsters was entirely a creation of the KGB. It existed only as long as the KGB allowed it to exist. The mafia contacted the director who authorized double what Connard asked for. Connard, of course, took it all. When he couldn't make the payment a year later, the mafia leaned on him, threatening to pour acid on his face. Harry was nothing if not vain. It was the worst fate he could imagine. The director sent Svetlana, now known as Mother, to offer Connard a deal.

"Mr. Connard, I represent the head office of Frontier Financing. I understand you are in arrears on your payments."

"Look, Miss whatever your name is, I'll get the money for you. I'm good for it. I'm a great business man. You can ask anyone, they'll tell you. You'll just have…"

Mother cut him off. "No, Harry, you are not a great business man. In fact, you are a blowhard and a disaster in business. But I am here to help you."

"So you'll give me an extension."

"Better than that. We'll hold the loan in abeyance until you can afford to pay it off. And we will continue to finance your company; in fact, we'll build up to a dozen new resorts for you."

Connard was skeptical. "And what do you get out of it?"

Mother paused, for effect, and explained to him, "We get twenty per cent of the profits and when we need your services, you provide them. Oh, and your company hires me as a consultant." She knew they would never see a ruble of profits, but it did not matter.

"And if I don't accept your offer? Who would I be providing services to?"

"You lose your one remaining resort and those gentlemen who explained what might happen to your face would be allowed to continue their job." She ignored the second question.

Connard cringed and accepted Mother's offer. It turned out he was her biggest find. While she had to continue to pour money into his operations, he used the money to buy fame and within ten years was a household name. Mother smiled every time she saw him on TV.

Over the next decade, she recruited a network of agents, mostly sleepers like Harry Connard. Some, like Anthony Payton, understood exactly what they were being asked to do and who their employer was. Others, like Brandon Jones, could care less who they were working for. They were just selling their skills, and, in Brandon's case, their passion for mayhem. Others, like Larry Gerstner, were in it only for the money. And there was a lot of money. In that time, Mother assembled a group of some forty agents. A few, like Brandon, did actual work. Most however were in places, or put in places, where they could be of service later.

As planned, the director of the KGB became president of Russia. His primary goal was to neutralize China and the United States, to bring their populaces under control of the Kremlin. He believed it was Russia's destiny to rule the world, and his destiny to rule Russia. He changed the name of the KGB to the FSB (Federal Security Bureau) and announced it would only deal with internal affairs. Everyone knew that was a lie, but no one challenged the statement. He divided the FSB into four groups: Internal Security, Industrial Espionage, American Desk, and China Desk. He personally supervised Mother and her three co-directors.

The president and Mother spent many long sessions developing a strategy for America. He favored a direct approach, but bowed to Mother's much better understanding of the American psyche.

"Mr. President, you must understand. Americans have way too much personal freedom. They are used to going where they want, when they want. While they can be led like sheep, they have to believe they are making their own decisions. We can use the media, especially the internet, to convince them of almost anything, especially now that they have willingly embraced ignorance as an easier choice, but they must believe they are controlling their own lives. Over a third of Americans own weapons. In fact, one tenth of those gun owners own 50% of the 300 million guns in the country. The only way we could avoid open warfare in the streets is if we could account at all times for every gun owner. Which sadly would mean we would have to account for every American."

The president remembered her concerns and called her two years later. "Recall, my Svetlana, our conversation about being able to account for every American if we are to control them?"

"Yes, sir."

The president boasted, "Our scientists have developed a nano GPS tracker, one so small you could hide a thousand in a thimble. All you have to do is figure out how to get the Americans tagged." Within a month, the brilliant mind of Mother had devised a plan. She flew to Paris where she made her way to a safe house at 3-5 *Rue d'Arras* on the second floor in the 5th arrondissement on the Left Bank. The area was touristy, but the spy world had discovered the utility of using websites like Airbnb and VRBO where one could rent any size quarters in any area for any time period with almost total anonymity. One paid in cash or with an untraceable bank transfer and blended into the general population. If you needed the place bugged or videoed, your team just rented the place before and after your rental. This spy business was so much easier these days.

The day after Mother's arrival, the Russian president flew in secretly to meet with her. She laid out her plan. The president nodded his head in approval, asked a few operational questions and then told her, "Before I approve this, you need to put my mind at ease about one of your sleepers."

"Yes, sir. Which one?"

"Harry Connard."

Mother furrowed her brow. "I'm not using him for anything other than for his organization which employs several of my people, myself included. We do run some money through his books, but nothing he knows about. He is pretty much a buffoon, and I'm not sure I would trust him for any real work. What is your concern?"

"His performances on television. His need for attention is so overwhelming; he will apparently say or do anything to get the camera on himself. I watched two nights ago when he was attacking the president of the United States, his own leader. After his appearance, the commentators discussed his viability as a potential candidate. We cannot have that. You have to shut him up."

Mother studied the president's face and thought about this problem. She did not immediately react. The president waited, his head tilted to the side, waiting for a response. Finally, Mother suggested, "Comrade President, perhaps the time has finally come. Perhaps it is the right moment for us to have our own presidential candidate." The president shook his head, but she persisted, "No, sir. Listen. He's a pompous fool, but he is smart enough to know he would have to do and say exactly as we demand. He has no chance of winning, but it would offer the opportunity for us to try out all of our theories on controlling a people who make their decisions based upon social networks and sound bites and their own uneducated beliefs. We can make his campaign offensive, just to test the limits." She paused to let the suggestion sink in, then continued, "Let's put the communication specialists on the America Desk to work on what this might look like. Will you agree to this?"

The president ran through her ideas in his mind and nodded his head slowly. "Put a plan together and let us look at it." She knew the "us" was the royal "us". She smiled.

EIGHTEEN

CUTTER

My appointment with Congresswoman Buday was set for the following Tuesday morning. Sandy had wanted to be briefed before the meeting, but I told her I still needed to work a few things out in my mind. She wasn't happy, but agreed to wait. The night preceding the meeting, I reviewed everything I had written down one last time, and decided maybe I was just being paranoid, looking for monsters under the bed. Christ in a hand basket. I told Sandy maybe we should cancel the meeting. She surprised me by saying, "No. There have been murmurs about AMASS and you need to talk to us."

I had shared my ideas with Rachel a few days before. She was not able to see what I was getting at. I think Rachel is perhaps the more likely to see the truth of things than anyone I ever met. She is the only person I would use the word "grok" to describe her ability to understand. When I typed "grok" it came up as a misspelling and yet it is one of the best words ever created. Robert A. Heinlein coined it and used it in *Stranger in a Strange Land*, for my money the best science fiction book ever written. To me it means the ability to go beyond understanding the facts, to see not just the meaning but the past, present and future of an idea. To feel what the facts mean to someone else. Pretty much the exact opposite of any thought our president ever had. So when Rachel didn't grok my paranoia, I started to doubt it.

The next morning, I fidgeted, notebook in hand, as I waited to be called in to see the congresswoman. Finally, I was summoned. I'd never been in an actual congressional office before and I was properly awed. Sandy told me to be seated while the congresswoman finished a call. I fidgeted some more. When the call ended, Congresswoman Buday turned to me and flashed her slightly crooked tooth smile. It was charming, and one of those little things which worked to her advantage politically. Old man Barney had told me as long as there were older male voters in her district, she would win because she looked just like Annette Funicello. Whoever that is.

"Yes, Mr. Williams, what can I do for you? Sandy tells me you have a, what to call it, a concern."

"Congresswoman Buday," I responded, but before I could get any further, she interrupted.

"Please call me Michele."

"Okay. And call me Cutter." I was immediately at ease. Good politicians could always do that. Make a person comfortable, make them feel important. Michele Buday was a good politician. I explained what I had seen. I started with the funny use of accounts and Cory's concern, to Cory's unlikely suicide, our involvement with KMI and the CDC and the missing numbers from our program.

Michele nodded and thought for a while after I finished. She turned to Sandy and asked, "What do you make of this?"

Sandy quickly replied, "I don't know. I had told Cutter about the intelligence community's non-belief in coincidence."

Michele turned back to me, "What do you make of it? Why do you think it may be something to worry about?"

I laid out my theory. "I think my boss may be selling our program off the books to either the CDC or FEMA, maybe some other Department of Defense agencies. I think Cory found out about it and someone killed him to keep him quiet. I think Marc is stealing from his partners, which would be of no concern to the government, but the money is coming in from numbered accounts which the government might be using illegally. I have no idea why they might want to use it off the record, or maybe they are trying to make their funding go further. It may not be illegal, but I just can't let the Cory thing go. I also would hate to see Marc screw over his partners."

Michele thought for a few minutes. "You know, Cutter, we deal with the folks in military intelligence, not the FBI. This might be more up their alley."

"I guess I'm just looking for direction or thoughts. Is this worth pursuing or am I just overreacting?"

"I'm not sure. Maybe the best thing to do is have someone who knows about ghosts under the bed talk to you." She turned to Sandy and asked her, "Could you call John Harris and see if he can get one of his guys to chat with Cutter? Off the record."

"Yes, ma'am." Sandy told her.

The congresswoman turned back to me, smiled that charming smile and asked, "Anything else we can do for you?" I shook my head no and before I knew it she was shaking my hand and gently guiding me to the door. As I left she told me, "It may take a while, but somebody will be in touch. Thank you so much for coming in," and the door closed behind me.

I waited at Sandy's desk until she came out. I asked her if this John Harris guy would be the person who calls me. She explained John wasn't a real person, it was a code name for their contact in the military intelligence community. "But you would like the guy, whatever his name is. He's chatty and always wants to tell me about his golf adventures."

I heard nothing over the next week or so. Some more numbers disappeared, but Rachel checked and no additional money came in or went out which she could not account for. Our friends at FEMA and the CDC continued the KM1 vaccinations, the Prez had gotten into more hot water when he publicly referred to the prime minister of England as a "pissant fart in the wind." The White House staff and the State Department worked overtime on damage control. The president decided he needed the high he could get only from cheering crowds, so he went on the road, holding a series of rallies to tout his success with the KM1 program. It was such old news, he got his cheering mobs, but no press coverage which mattered.

It was the end of March and business was slow at the office. Marc called us together and told us he had earned a vacation and was going to St. Martin for three weeks. I'd never been there. I'd heard they have a terrific nude beach, but no golf. I decided I must be getting old if golf was more appealing than bare boobs. On Marc's first day away, the office felt entirely different, like it was breathing a huge sigh of relief. We didn't realize how much tension

Marc created constantly. I celebrated by ordering pizza for everyone at lunch. We ended up turning it into a party, complete with beer and wine and exactly zero work got done all afternoon. It was the best day at AMASS since Cory was there.

I thought about the day as I drove home and realized maybe it was the tension I felt at work which made me suspect nefarious goings-on. The folks at AMASS were a good group of work mates, we had actually helped with a national crisis, and we all were being paid handsomely. I gave Maria the night off and took the kids and Sandy out to dinner at a local restaurant whose specialty is ice cream. I got two big smiles and one shaking head. Sandy did ask if I'd heard from anyone about my concerns and I told her not yet.

A few days later, I got an email from Lowry Raleigh, even though his office was no more than twenty feet from mine. It was so like Lowry, precise, noncommittal and impersonal. I'd worked with him for a long time and yet knew almost nothing about him. In fact, while he did speak the language of manpower management eloquently, I'd never heard him speak anything else. I remembered giving him and the other partners an outline for a new operations manual. He told me he would look at it and let me know. Marc approved the changes, we made the switchover and six months later Lowry told me it might work and we should give it a test run. After that I kind of exchanged only pleasantries with him when appropriate. And a few times made client calls with him.

Lowry wanted me to go on a client call at the Army Corps of Engineers. Since they were originally one of my clients, I had to agree. Though I knew how it would go. We'd arrive, exchange greetings, then he and the engineers would tech speak for a couple of hours, we would exchange "thank yous" and Lowry and I would go to his favorite restaurant. We'd eat at Ping Pong Dim Sum where Lowry would have the crispy chicken with orange glaze, the only thing he ever ordered. At the end of the meal, he would pat all his pockets and announce he had forgotten his wallet and ask me to buy lunch. Which I always did.

This trip was exactly the same, except for one little detail. When he patted his pockets, he actually found a wallet in his breast pocket. He opened it and handed it to me. It contained but one thing (sadly, not money, so I was buying lunch yet again), a military ID with Lowry's name and photograph on it. It identified him as a Major in the U.S. Army and had his DoD identification number. There was no date on the expiration date line. I read it all twice.

When I looked up, it was not the Lowry face I was used to seeing, the one that was open and friendly and always looked a little befuddled. This face was stern and almost menacing. Then it smiled and Lowry reached his hand across the table. I shook it while he said, "Lowry Raleigh, Major, United States Army. I understand from John Harris you have some concerns about our boss and our company?"

I was flabbergasted. It didn't make any sense. "You know John Harris?" I asked, a bit incredulous.

Lowry continued to smile. "Well, no one really knows John Harris. He's more of a catchall for several people. I take it you have been told John Harris exists. And you are expecting a visit from his representative?" I nodded my head. "So I'm here. Tell me what you know and think."

I wondered about several things. If John Harris was the name applied to faceless military intelligence people, and Lowry was one of them, why was he at AMASS and wouldn't he already know about the things I knew? Which would mean I was in fact seeing evil plots where none existed. I felt foolish. I decided to test the ground before I walked into someplace I could not walk out of.

"I'm sorry, Lowry, but I'm very confused. I thought you were a part owner of AMASS and your job was being our manpower specialist. You're the guy who makes the software program mean something to users. What am I missing here?" I asked him, but I was thinking I must be missing the boat. Or some marbles.

"The back story. You're missing the back story. Which I suppose I should share."

"Please."

Lowry told me his story. He was a ROTC lieutenant right out of college when he was assigned to the military police. Turned out he had a nose for investigation. He liked it and was good at it. It didn't take him long to discover his niche. One of the biggest thefts in any organization is the theft of time—employees who are misused or allowed to misuse their time. Lowry's assignment was to go into army agencies and root out this loss of resources. He found everything from a general using his troops in his own private million-dollar business to whole battalions doing nothing at all.

About twenty-five years before, he was a captain doing undercover work at the Rock Island Arsenal when he was approached by Marc Payton and Norman Pidgeon about joining them in a business venture. He politely declined, but they kept pursuing him. He reported what had happened to his superiors who saw an opportunity, as well as a way to monitor a potential problem. I asked him to explain.

"Cutter, you know about Anthony, Marc's twin brother, right?" I nodded. "When Anthony was released by the army, there were more than a few concerns about him because of what he went through. The army decided having someone close to his brother might tip us off to any developing problem."

"Like what kind of problem?"

"We thought he was mentally unstable. Of course he died later, but I stayed at AMASS because my superiors also reasoned the position I had been offered would allow me to go into military agencies and do undercover work, ask all the kinds of questions we wanted to and it would all be in the guise of doing work for a contractor. Turned out my superiors were correct. I do the work for not just the army, but for any branch of the military or any agency the military wishes to help."

"And the persona you use?" I asked.

Lowry grinned. "Cutter, you'd be surprised what secrets people will tell the Lowry you know. He is entirely hapless and guileless. Makes him trustworthy." He shrugged his shoulders. "Now, tell me what your concerns are."

"I have one more question, kind of personal. Does the army pay you in addition to what you get at AMASS?"

He laughed and shook his head, "You won't believe this, but I have to turn in all of my AMASS earnings to the army. Wasn't a problem until you came along and our income soared. Each month it gets tougher and tougher to give up all that money. But it's my job."

I shared with him all of my concerns, from Cory to the missing numbers. Naturally he knew about some of it, the use of the accounts and he'd heard a rumor about the missing numbers. He did not know about the email from Cory which I shared with him. He did not know about the fight Cory had with Marc right before he left. He did not know about money from numbered accounts.

"So am I just being paranoid? Being stupid?"

"I don't know. Let me think about it and maybe run a few things by John Harris. But don't mention any of this to anyone." I suppose he thought I was agreeing by my not saying anything, but I knew I had to tell Rachel. And maybe Sandy. We left the restaurant and by the time we got on the Metro, Lowry was back in character. He had lost his Metro pass and I had to buy him his fare back to the office.

The following morning, I met Rachel for breakfast and told her all about my lunch with Lowry. Like me, she was floored. "Let me get this straight, Cutter, Lowry Raleigh is some kind of spy and not just what he seems to be." She was rightfully stunned.

"Not exactly a spy. He's more of an undercover cop. When I thought about it, it made more sense. He really doesn't socialize at all with folks in the office, he spends lots of time on site with clients and he seems to produce very little for the company. Sure explains a lot of that."

"So what did he make of your theory?"

"Said he'd think about it and talk to his folks in the army. He tried to appear neutral, but I got the feeling he had the same reaction as you." She raised her eyebrows as a question. "He thinks I'm a flake as well."

"That's not what I said. I just don't see any connection. I wasn't as close to Cory as you were and am more likely to believe it was a suicide." She paused, then asked, "What now?"

"Nothing, I guess. Wait and see if Lowry does anything with it."

"If he doesn't, will you try some other path?"

"You know, like my daddy always said, 'If at first you don't succeed, quit. Don't make an ass of yourself.'" I gave Rachel my best aw-shucks smile and she rolled her eyes.

I decided to tell Sandy and she had an entirely different reaction. I did not tell her who the contact was, but only that I had met with a member of army intelligence. I explained I thought the guy wasn't too impressed with my story. She said to let her know because she and the congresswoman did not want to let it lie without action. I almost got the feeling they were looking for political ammunition. Before I could say anything, Sandy added, "Cutter, I think we need to talk."

I've heard that phrase more times than I would like to think about. It is never something you want to hear, but I guess I have become inured to it. My response was, "So talk."

"I think I have to start spending a lot more time away from the house. Stephen is pressuring me and I can't give up what I have with him. I just can't." She paused for some reaction or comment from me. I had none, so she continued. "I'll be here for the kids three nights a week, but not Monday through Thursday. I know it may not be the best solution, but you have Maria and lots of times

166

I'm not here when they go to bed anyway." She waited for a minute or two and added, "So what do you think?"

What do I think? Does it matter one fucking bit what I think? I think you want to eat your cake and have it too. I think you are seriously fucked up. I think you have a very strange view of family. I think Stephen Scott is in for a big surprise when you decide you're done with him, and you are in for one when you try to come home. I think, Mrs. Sandra Elizabeth Surface (Morton) Williams, you have serious issues you should deal with and I think you may be the biggest mistake I ever made. I think you should get the hell out of our lives and never come back.

What I said was, "Sandy, you need to do what you need to do. You do none us any good by pretending to feel or be something you aren't. We'll explain to Jordan and Livingston it's your job to be away. You and I, I hope we can stay friendly, if not friends. And good luck, but you know this will be the end of us, right?"

She looked down and said quietly, "I know. I'm sorry. I truly am."

Take your "sorry" and stuff it up your ass. Though in truth I was happy to have it all over and done with. I could get on with my life.

A week later Lowry stopped at my desk and asked if I would take a walk with him. The weather was unusually cold for mid-April so I asked if we could just go get coffee instead. He shook his head and told me we had to talk outside. I grabbed my coat and followed him into the street. We walked up Washington towards King Street. He looked straight ahead and spoke quietly. "My folks think we need to look deeper into this. You'll have to help us."

"What did they say?"

"I called the authorities in Spain about Cory's suicide. The detective in charge of the case told me the official report ruled it was a suicide."

"But?" I asked.

"But I asked the detective what he thought and he told me '*Huele a pescado*'." I asked Lowry what that meant. He told me, "The literal translation is 'it smells like fish'. The guy thinks it was an expertly staged murder."

"Why does he think that?"

"Apparently the gun used would be impossible for someone like Cory to acquire. It is sold only to law enforcement agencies, and if you could get one on the black market, it would cost you thousands. If you could. Why would a guy spend thousands to put one bullet in his own head? He wouldn't."

"What are you going to do?"

He told me his plan.

NINETEEN

CUTTER

Lowry figured the only way to expose any misdealing was to attack it not from the AMASS side but from the client side. He decided we would pick three or four of our largest clients and do surprise on-site inspections, thinking if our team showed up, it might just shake something loose. We would take a small trustworthy group. And not share with Marc. Marc would be told we were going one place for something entirely different while we would actually be at one of our client's. After some discussion, we decided the team would be Lowry and I, Rachel and Mary Beth. Lowry chose the clients: Corps of Engineers (our largest), FEMA, the CDC and National Parks, in that order. Lowry told me Rachel and Mary Beth were not to know about either the real purpose of the trips or about his true role. He would stay in character for the trips. Not just for our coworkers, but also for the innocent clients.

I agreed, but once again I knew I would be telling Rachel. I figured if I couldn't trust her, all was lost anyway. It was actually kind of exciting, being part of a sting operation, one that might tell me what happened to Cory. And, I have to admit, a little scary since Cory had died. Of course, he didn't have a military cop with him like I would have.

We made travel arrangements outside of the office, had team meetings at lunch and were ready to start the following Monday. The Thursday before news started coming in slowly of a problem with an anti-vaccination group in the Midwest. According to the first sketchy reports, several different militias had joined together and taken over a large farm outside of Granville, Ohio. The spokesman, Dave Gilmore, who referred to himself as Doctor David Gilmore, though no one could find any evidence of him being a doctor of any kind, proclaimed his group outside control of the federal government and, therefore, could not be required to be vaccinated. He welcomed anyone who agreed to join them.

The CDC filed an injunction against them which was quickly granted. Dr. Gilmore held a press conference and announced, "We represent 2,000 men, women and children all of whom know their constitutional rights to refuse this so-called medicine. We will defend those rights by whatever means are necessary. To a person, we supported President Connard and his efforts to return this great country to what it was when it was founded: free, white and God-fearing. We are asking President Connard to intercede on our behalf and stop this terrible injustice. Do it, Mr. President, for everyone who supported you."

By the weekend the story flooded all of the media. Sunday afternoon, apparently worried about losing his already shrinking base, the president held a press conference and announced his support for the group and ordered the CDC to back off. The country went wild. All those who had been vaccinated against their will threatened to sue the government. The program, mid stride, stopped nationwide. Monday morning, just as we were entering the offices of the Army Corps of Engineers, the president called another press conference and reversed field, ordering the Granville

Battalion, as they called themselves, to step down and allow for the inoculation of their members. They refused and challenged the government to "do something about it."

We spent three days at the Corps and found exactly diddley squat. Clean books, clean software, clean application, no record of any stolen numbers. We had shaken nothing loose. We crossed them off the list and decided to go to FEMA on Friday when we might be the least expected. Lowry had shared with me he believed if there was a culprit out there somewhere, FEMA was the most likely candidate. I had asked him why and he told me within government circles, FEMA was considered a renegade. While it was a part of the Department of Homeland Security, it in fact answered only to the president. They made their own rules and they ran their operations as a paramilitary organization. They were, in a word, untrusted.

We showed up at FEMA headquarters just south of the National Mall Friday morning at 8:00. We were met at the door by a half dozen heavily armed guards and told no one was allowed into headquarters that morning. The agency was on full alert and in close down mode. We were instructed to call to find out when we would be allowed in. We were given no reason and we returned to the AMASS office. Lowry told me on the Metro he believed they had seen us coming, somehow, and most likely FEMA was our guilty party. He was as excited as I had seen him. He said he would take the rest of the day off and chase down the lead with his guys. Turned out that was not the reason at all.

When we got back to the office, everyone there was gathered around the television, or watching on their computers. FEMA and

CDC employees, with a contingent of ATF and National Guard, had tried to enter the Granville Battalion farm. When the ATF agents began to force their way through the fortified gates at the entry to the farm, Granville Battalion guards opened fire. Turned out the Battalion was heavily armed, not just with fully automatic rifles but also with stinger missiles and truck mounted high caliber machine guns. They decimated the government troops and suffered few casualties to their own. The government withdrew, carrying out twenty dead and over fifty injured. We watched it all on live TV. It felt like the start of a civil war.

The Ohio National Guard was on the scene within hours, 5,000 strong. Granville, four miles to the north, was evacuated as was the surrounding area. Helicopters were sent to patrol the airspace above and one was shot down immediately. The others withdrew. The president made no statements, in fact he could not be found. All weekend long it was a standoff. The Democrats in Congress took to the airwaves, calling for action by the administration. My friend Michele Buday was interviewed on three Sunday morning public affairs shows. She basically declared war on the president.

Monday morning the governor of Ohio called for the peaceful surrender of the Granville Battalion. Dr. Gilmore told the governor to "go fuck yourself. President Connard will back us up." Midafternoon, the president finally showed his face, looking worse for the wear. In an unusually terse statement, he gave the Battalion three hours to surrender, with promises of immunity. Gilmore announced Connard was no longer his president. At 7:00 in the evening, the National Guard opened fire. Three hours later it was all over, except for carrying out all the body bags, which ran into the hundreds. The rebellion was over. An overnight poll showed the president's approval rating had dropped to twelve percent.

By Wednesday, the stock market had lost ten percent of its value. First the liberal news media, then the Democrats in Congress called for the president's resignation. Connard tried to hold a rally of his supporters and was booed from the stage. The country, all of us at AMASS included, was numb. I had not heard from Sandy since Sunday morning, though she had called the kids. Friday we tried to enter FEMA again and were told to come back the following week. We did, and found nothing out of the ordinary. FEMA was just as clean as the Corps of Engineers. Lowry was dejected.

It was time to take the show to Atlanta. Since we would be out of town and didn't want to alert Marc, or anyone else, Rachel and Mary Beth were listed as "on vacation", Lowry was to be missing in action and I was supposedly going to Jacksonville for a client visit. The team met at Reagan National and flew into Hartsfield Monday morning. We spent the day reviewing plans, though they were the same as our previous visitations. Mary Beth wanted to call Julie for dinner, but Lowry told her no. Rachel and I took in the aquarium and had a nice dinner.

After dinner we stopped at the lobby bar for a nightcap. I decided it was time to tell her about the home front. "Rachel, I don't know what this all means yet, but Sandy has moved out, at least for four nights a week. She comes home on Friday after work to spend the weekend with the kids, to pretend to be a family. And I let her. Pretty fucked up, huh?"

Rachel set her scotch down on our small drink table and pulled her chair over next to mine. She took my hand and squeezed it. "Cutter, you can't ask me a question like that. I don't know what's best for you or for your kids. You know how I feel about you. Or you should. I want you to be happy, but I can't be more than friends with you as it is. No pressure. I'm very happy with my life right now and I don't see getting into a messy situation to screw that up." She picked up her scotch and held it up to me in a toast. I clinked her glass with my bourbon and she said, "To both our happinesses" and she smiled. She made me feel a lot warmer inside than the bourbon did.

Tuesday, bright and early, we showed up at the front door of the Center for Disease Control. We were told to be seated in the lobby, and within two minutes Julie Barney was there greeting us. She did not seem the least bit surprised, in fact, it was like she was waiting for us. I glared at Mary Beth and she frowned and shook her head to let me know she hadn't told. Julie took us back to her area where Larry Gerstner stood waiting for us.

"Dr. Gerstner," I said reaching my hand out to shake. "We've been seeing lots of you on television. Very impressive, what you've done."

"Thanks," he said, shaking my hand firmly. "Just part of the job," but his smile indicated he was pretty happy with the attention. "So what brings you down our way? Problems?"

"No," I told him. "Just routine system check." I introduced him to Rachel and Lowry whom he had not met. I laid out what all we were going to look at and what we were trying to accomplish. Except that last part of course was a lie. I got to the part about looking through the numbers they had used and he held up his hand.

"Ah, you caught us at a bad time. We do our routine run-throughs on Tuesday, so can that wait until tomorrow, or so we don't screw up your schedule, maybe this evening around five?"

I looked at my teammates and they all nodded it was okay with them. We spent until two doing what we could, broke for a late lunch and told Julie we would be back at five. When we returned, we were met by a young man in a lab coat who apologized to us, "Sorry, but Dr. Gerstner and Julie got delayed for about ninety minutes. They asked me if I might give you a tour of our facilities. Would that be all right with you folks?"

I noticed Lowry check his watch but I told the kid, "Sure. That's fine. Lead on, MacDuff." I forget serious young scientists don't read a lot of Shakespeare, or more correctly, misread it.

"I'm sorry. My name is Todd." Todd looked confused.

"Sorry, Todd. Please lead the way."

"We'll start with the U.S. Quarantine Station, our largest and most advanced station in the country." He led us across the campus to an imposing building which looked like it was under the tightest security.

Before we went in, Mary Beth hesitated and asked, "Is it safe?"

"The parts you will be allowed into are probably the cleanest and safest rooms you can find outside of a lab. You'll be perfectly fine."

Todd showed us the intake center where visitors to the country who were diagnosed with a disease or thought to possibly be carrying a disease were registered. He led us through a labyrinth of labs and observation cells where what he described as their "guests" were kept. The section which was currently occupied was off limits to us. Thankfully. About an hour into our tour which, frankly, was pretty damned boring, Todd excused himself to take a phone call. He stepped down the hall we were in and spoke for about a minute. When he rejoined us he said, "That was Dr. Gerstner. He said I should show you the primary lab here and he would meet us there."

"Lead on, Todd," I said, trying to be clever. It went unnoticed.

He took us down an elevator to a level called 4SB, which I assumed meant the fourth sub-basement. When we stepped off, we immediately noticed much cooler air and a faint medicinal odor. The place was white concrete and white tile and looked completely antiseptic. Todd held the door of the elevator as we stepped out and said, "Dr. Gerstner will be here in a few. Thanks for letting me show you around." He stepped back into the elevator and the door closed.

We wandered into the cavernous room, making our way over to where there were several tables and some plastic-covered couches and chairs. We sat to wait. Maybe ten minutes later, the elevator door opened and a guy several years older, but in much better shape than me, walked toward us. He had a crew cut and a military bearing. Before he could introduce himself, Lowry stood and said, "Brandon, what are you doing here?"

I turned to Lowry and asked, "You know him?"

"Yes, I do. He's a friend of Marc's."

TWENTY

MOTHER

Like everyone else in America, Mother watched the news coming out of Granville, Ohio. Unlike most everyone else, Mother smiled. This was just the kind of idiot behavior which was going to cost Americans their country and the control of their lives. She had always admired how the arms manufacturers of the world had usurped the original purpose of the NRA and used it to insure they would always have a ready supply of customers. In America alone, not counting military and police spending, over ten billion dollars were spent annually on guns and ammunition. How did they do it? By convincing people that which they held most sacred (but did not understand), the United States Constitution, said everyone could own as many guns of any kind they wanted and that there were evil forces who would take that right away from them. They would lose their ability to fight tyranny. A crock, but a crock which worked.

What Mother had told the president of Russia was here on display. A small group of heavily armed malcontents was waging war on their government. Imagine what would happen if a foreign government tried to take control of the country. It wouldn't just be a few malcontents. It would be every gun owner out there. Her plan to identify and track those gun owners in order to neutralize them when necessary would be crucial to any takeover.

Mother erupted in a rare display of anger when she watched as her President Connard announced the paramilitary group would not have to be vaccinated. These were the people she most needed to be able to track. What the hell is he thinking? Why does he even believe he can think? Within hours, the entire program was at risk. For what? To satisfy that asshole's need for adulation? She texted him a coded message.

Seven hours later, President Connard stood before her in her apartment. "Harry, your actions today were beyond stupid. My boss wants me to cancel our contract," she lied. Connard knew what "cancel our contract" meant. His only relief was knowing if they were canceling his contract, they wouldn't tell him. He would just be dead.

"I'm sorry, Mother. I didn't think it through. What can I do to fix it?"

"Go back on television tomorrow and reverse your order. We have vaccinated less than half the population and we need it finished and we need it finished soon. Make sure every one of those militia are vaccinated or dead. Do you understand?"

"Yes, ma'am." He paused, then sheepishly added, "Is there anything else I should do?"

"Two things. One, never do anything that interferes with this program again, and, two, get the fuck out of my sight." Harry almost ran down the hall in retreat.

A couple of days later, Mother watched as government forces overwhelmed and subdued the Granville Battalion. She knew what she had told her boss was true: if the populace had guns, they would believe they could fight off any foreign intruder. The fact they could see on television how futile and wasteful such action would be did not dissuade them. No armed populace could stand up to a trained military force, no matter how many automatic weapons they had stashed in their basements. What was even more amazing was these Americans were willing to put up with mass killings of school kids to protect a right which was useless to them. Ignorance did truly rule the country.

Friday afternoon, Mother received a call from her contact at FEMA. The agent told her about representatives of AMASS showing up unannounced to do an inspection on the tracking software. While FEMA was not using it for anything other than employees, the agent thought Mother should know in case they were headed to the CDC. Mother took down all the information, including who was part of the team. She called Marc Payton.

"Mr. Payton, can you tell me why your employees are doing a system check at FEMA?"

"What? What are you talking about?"

"Four of your employees are at FEMA doing some kind of audit on the use of your software by FEMA. Luckily we are not using it there, but if you guys are doing audits everywhere, they'll find out what's going on at the CDC."

"Do you know who is there?"

Mother gave him the list of Williams, Raleigh, Red Cloud and Irelan.

Marc told her, "Hold on. Let me check." Two minutes later he was back on the phone. "Your contacts must be mistaken. Those four are working on a problem at the Department of Treasury."

Mother was quiet long enough to make Marc nervous. Finally, she told him, "If you can't control your staff, maybe you are in the wrong position. We cannot afford a screw up on this. Find out what they are doing, where they are going and when. *Capiche?*"

Marc checked the work schedules for the next couple of weeks, found that Cutter was going to Jacksonville and Mary Beth and Rachel were to be on vacation. As usual, Lowry had not turned in a schedule. He called Mother back and told her no one was scheduled to go to the CDC, or anywhere close to Atlanta. He assured her he would not let that happen.

Mother did not leave things to chance. She hated having to rely on other people, especially people who would sell out their own countrymen. It was the single biggest danger to what otherwise was the perfect plan. When her president had given her the nano GPS technology, the only challenge was a delivery system. She had long ago made arrangements for a tracking system—she had stolen AMASS by substituting Anthony Payton for his brother. Her technical staff tried a couple of ideas to get the nano technology implanted and finally hit upon putting the GPS units into an injectable serum. Mother herself had come up with the idea of an epidemic which would throw the country into a panic and make everyone demand to be inoculated with the serum.

It took the better part of a year to create enough doses for the entire American population. Her president wanted to see how it worked in the United States, and if it was successful, he was going to use it on his own people. Each dose contained several hundred GPS units, each with the same ID number. Tests had shown some would be lost to normal bodily functions, but some would remain in the blood stream, and some would become permanently lodged in organs such as the liver or kidney. The United States government had been thoughtful enough to make sure everyone had an ID number assigned to them. A number folks readily accepted because it would provide them money for retirement. They even called it Social Security, as in state security. The GPS ID number would be linked to the Social Security number, and with the Social Security number, they could find out anything they wanted about the citizen. Anything.

Mother was so close she could feel the power surging through her. Another few months, every American tagged and traceable, and a president she owned in a country doomed by its own ignorance. The Americans had had everything at their disposal to create perhaps the greatest society in the history of man. They got too greedy and too lazy. Instead of taking care of the less fortunate, they fed on them. Mother had grown to like many of these people and was in a way sorry to see this happen. But she believed what she was doing would ultimately be the best for her country and humanity.

While she hoped Marc was right and it was just a communications screw up, Mother called Larry Gerstner and told him what had happened at FEMA, warned him to be on the lookout for visitors, any visitors, from AMASS.

"I've got it covered, Mother," he told her. "If they show up, what should we do?"

"Stall them and call me. Do not, I repeat, do not let them do any number checking."

Gerstner tried to assure her, "You needn't worry. Julie has set up the system to take random ID numbers from AMASS storage. They have no way of checking it, nor can they gain access to our data storage servers. Their system is completely bypassed. Julie set it up as an identical system, but there is no way they can access it. It's foolproof."

Mother thought for almost a minute before she responded. "You know, Lawrence, I don't believe in foolproof. These are smart people. If they come they will be looking for something, anything. We don't know what they are after or why. Might be something having nothing to do with us. It's not like they have the FBI with them. But stall them and call me. And keep your ears open."

The following Tuesday morning Gerstner called Mother. "You were right. They're here, down in the lobby right now. We'll stall as much as we can but then what?"

"See if you can find out what they're looking for and let me know."

Two hours later, Julie Barney asked Mary Beth to take a break and go get coffee with her. After they were alone Julie asked her, "So what's the deal with this inspection, or review or whatever it is? We do something wrong?"

Mary Beth said, "Oh, no, it's just that we're missing some random numbers. Cutter seems to think they are being stolen. I've tried to tell him it is probably just some kind of bug, but he wants to check. You're the third client we've been to, and I'm sure we won't find anything here either." She smiled and lowered her voice. "So, what's with you and Dr. Gerstner? Tell."

Now Julie smiled. "Oh, God, he is so great. I'm crazy about him. It's a secret, so you can't say anything, but after we get through this KM1 treatment program, we're going to get married. A big wedding, like I've always wanted. It's so perfect." Her voice trailed off. Mary Beth congratulated her and they returned to the others.

As soon as she could, Julie pulled Larry aside and told him what she had learned and assured him the AMASS folks could not find what they had been doing. He squeezed her hand and told the group he needed to check in on a few things in his office. He called Mother and told her what they had learned. Mother told Larry she was sending Brandon to fix the problem in spite of his objection. Mother almost whispered, "No, Lawrence, we'll do this my way. Get them isolated in a safe place and Brandon will take over. Get yourself and that Barney woman far away from the office and someplace where you will have an alibi. And say nothing but 'yes, ma'am'."

"Yes, ma'am."

Mother then called Marc and told him, in fact, his employees and partners were out of control. She would deal with it, but he needed to figure out what had gone wrong and fix it. She was not pleasant with him.

She then called Brandon Jones and ordered him to Atlanta.

TWENTY-ONE

CUTTER

I'm not sure, maybe because of the tone of voice Cory had used when he mentioned Brandon's name, but for some reason little alarm bells went off in my head when he first walked in. Brandon Jones did not look one bit like I expected. I would have thought him to be a little weasley guy and this man was the commandant straight out of a Pat Conroy book. He walked quickly over to where our group was seated and addressed Lowry who had stood to greet him.

Lowry repeated his question, "What brings you here? Message from Marc?"

Brandon smiled, but it was not what you would call a heartwarming smile. "You could say that, I guess." By now the rest of us had stood. I offered my hand and he shook it and said, "Mr. Williams," then turned toward the women and bowed his head slightly and said, "Ms. Red Cloud, Ms. Irelan." He stepped back a couple of paces.

"I'm going to need for you folks to come with me."

"Why?" Lowry asked, letting his voice slip into his military police persona.

"You'll learn soon enough."

Lowry's demeanor had now changed enough to confuse Mary Beth. "I don't think so," he answered and he shifted his weight back onto his heels as if digging in.

The video stored in my head of the ensuing seconds or minutes or hours runs at various speeds at different times. Sometimes it goes so fast I cannot see it, but I know it is there. Other times, it is slow motion slowed even more, like a replay to see if a player stepped out of bounds. As I watched Lowry and tried to understand what was going on, Brandon moved to Rachel's side and put his thumb and forefinger on the sides of her neck. When she pulled away, he squeezed hard enough for her to cry out. He then got his left arm around her throat and pulled her into his body. I looked at her face. She did not appear scared. She looked belligerent.

I could not control my reaction. I turned and started to lunge at Brandon. Only then did I notice the long barreled gun in Brandon's hand. He raised it in my direction, and I was looking down the barrel into a black hole which appeared to be wide enough for a golf ball. I froze two feet short of him, the reaction Brandon was looking for.

I remember a line, an image, from a western I read as a kid, maybe Zane Grey, maybe Louis L'Amour. It went something like, "The six-gun flashed into Tex's hand and spat out two quick bursts of fire, the sound deafening." I can see how a writer would come up with that description, though in person it happens so much slower. While my eyes were focused on the hole in the end of that gun barrel, in my peripheral vision, a pistol appeared in Lowry's hand as if by magic, he slowly raised it and before Brandon could react, shot him once in the head.

I had never seen anyone die in my life, not at their bedside or in an accident or ever. I had never even been the one to find a body.

The only time I had seen a dead person was wrapped up neatly in a coffin. I saw Brandon die. I saw the shine go out in his eyes. It seemed to take forever, but he just dropped to the floor. The sound had been deafening, but was quickly drowned out by Mary Beth screaming. The color had drained from Rachel's face and I got to her before she collapsed. I held her and felt her shake. Lowry was yelling at us, but the words were garbled.

Finally, the ringing in my ears stopped and I was able to make out what Lowry was saying. "Listen, all of you. You have to be quiet and we have to get out of here. We don't know if there are other people here after us or not. I need to call the police, but there is no reception down here." Mary Beth turned and ran toward the elevator until Lowry yelled at her to stop. "We can't use the elevator. It was security card activated. There has to be an emergency exit somewhere."

We followed him through a doorway on the side of the huge room and down a corridor, leaving Brandon Jones in a heap on the floor. The hallway was lined with offices or labs, all white tile behind reinforced glass. The corridor appeared to be a dead end, but at its end was a smaller hallway to the left and at the end of it was an exit sign. We heard a commotion behind us and Mary Beth halted and turned toward the noise. Lowry grabbed her arm and pulled her along. The stairs behind the exit door went both up and down, but up was where freedom was, as well as phone reception.

We got to the main floor, completely out of breath and exited into the main hallway. There was no one in sight except the security guard at the main entrance. I noticed Lowry had the gun

186

in his hand behind his back as we approached the guard. The guard looked at us quizzically but showed no alarm. Lowry spoke to him, "We need the police. Do you have a direct line?"

"Yessir, but it's for emergencies only."

Lowry flashed his ID at the man and ordered, "Call them and tell them there has been a shooting." A brief look of panic crossed the guard's face, but he did as he was told. We sat down and waited for the cops to arrive. Half a dozen cars, lights flashing, were there within five minutes. Lowry placed his weapon between his feet on the floor and he instructed us to all show our hands, palms forward, as the police came in. We did as we were told.

Lowry identified himself and explained what had happened. Several police officers had the guard take them downstairs to see the body, several more started a sweep of the building and three detectives separated us and interviewed us independently. Except Mary Beth who had gone into shock and was taken to an emergency room in the main CDC building. We gave our statements and were released. It was midnight.

Rachel, Lowry and I rode back to the hotel in silence. They had decided to keep Mary Beth for observation. When we walked in to the hotel, Lowry said to us, "Listen you two, go to your rooms, lock the doors and don't come out until you hear from me." Then to me, with a slight smile, "It appears you had already filled Rachel in." I started to protest, but he held up his hand. "It's okay. Turns out it was probably better for her to know." He paused. "Looks like we kicked something loose. And it looks like you were right about Cory. Sadly, our only lead is pretty much dead. That leaves us Marc. And Dr. Gerstner. My guys are flying in and I'll meet with them as soon as they get here. Again, don't leave your rooms until you hear from me."

Rachel spoke, "Lowry, thank you for saving our lives." She said nothing else.

"Go on, you two, get some sleep. We'll have a long day tomorrow."

We rode up the elevator without speaking. When we got to Rachel's door, she said quietly, "Would you come in for a few minutes 'til I fall asleep? I don't want to be alone."

"Sure," I said and followed her in. I went directly to the mini bar where I got us a gin and a scotch. We sat for a few minutes quietly before Rachel spoke.

"What do you think it all means?"

"It means something is badly wrong at AMASS or the CDC or both. I suppose we'll find out when Lowry finishes with his guys. At least, I hope we do."

Rachel seemed to think about that for a couple of minutes, then, "Will you sit here while I take a shower and get ready for bed?"

"Sure. As long as you buy me another gin." She smiled, got up, retrieved me another baby bottle of gin and went into the bathroom. Ten minutes later she emerged, wrapped in a terrycloth robe way too large for her, hair damp and plastered to her head. I got up to leave.

"Will you stay?"

"No. But I'll come back." I went to my room, brushed my teeth, changed into my comfortable jeans and tee shirt, perfect for chair sleeping, and was back in her room within five minutes.

188

Rachel Red Cloud was lying on the bed in a long sleeve tee shirt that came to her knees. It had the logo of the Jake, the special event we had both worked on several years ago. It made me laugh. She patted the bed and asked, "Will you hold me until I go to sleep?" I held her until we were both asleep. Or at least until I was asleep, which took about 2.5 seconds.

I half awoke when there was a little light showing around the drapes. I felt Rachel's strong back against my chest and her deep and slow breathing. I smelled soap and shampoo mingled with her own scent. I reached down and pulled her tee shirt slowly up so I could slide my hand onto her bare stomach. I caressed her stomach then moved my hand up to her breasts. I knew what the rules were and I knew I was breaking them, but I figured if she awoke and objected, I could feign doing it in my sleep and beg forgiveness. Easier to ask forgiveness than permission. I felt wrongly male but I moved my hand down her stomach and into her underwear and she made a small sound and pressed closer to me.

I touched her for a short time, then removed her clothes and explored every part of her body with my hands and mouth. She returned the favor, took off my shirt and jeans and explored me. Explored me to the point I thought I would explode.

She rolled on top of me and I held her by the shoulders and spoke for the first time, "Are we safe, you know, birth control?" She finally smiled and eased herself down onto me. She moved, slowly and then more quickly. She was absolutely quiet, not something I was used to. She moved faster and then stopped for a few seconds, her shoulders tensing then relaxing below my fingers.

She soon started moving again, very slowly. After a couple of minutes, she rolled us over and I could no longer control myself and finished. It was the most intense experience I'd ever had.

We lay together until our breathing returned to normal and then for several minutes more. Rachel finally spoke. "I'm starved. Order us some breakfast." I smiled and rolled over, grabbed the room phone and called room service.

"Hi. This is room 319 and we'd like to order some breakfast."

"I'm sorry, sir. We stopped serving breakfast at 11:00, though we could make you some scrambled eggs and toast."

"That would be perfect. For two. With coffee and lots of orange juice."

"Very good, sir. It will be to your room in about thirty minutes."

While I was on the phone, Rachel had made her way into the bathroom and returned. I excused myself, used the bathroom and then we were back in bed, Rachel demurely in the tee shirt I had been wearing, me substantially less demure in my birthday suit.

"You are not at all like I expected you to be," she said.

I raised my eyebrows. "What did you expect?" thinking I had disappointed her.

"I don't know. You were sexier." She stopped, then started again, "Not sexier. That's not the right word. You made me feel sexier. You are..." and her voice trailed off. "You know, I have never had two orgasms before. And never one where I was on the bottom. How did you do that? And how did you know I liked mornings better?"

I smiled and said nothing. I had no idea about how any of that happened, but I figured silence would allow me to take credit for all of it. We were quiet for a while. I told her, "I love you, you know."

She put a finger to my lips and said, "I know. But let's not talk about it." Before I could respond or argue, there was a knock at the door and the room phone rang at the same instant. I pointed to the door and Rachel answered the phone. I pulled on my jeans and got our breakfast from the bellhop. He got a 100 per cent tip, because, what the hell, it was on Rachel's tab, which was on AMASS's tab, which meant Marc was paying for most of it.

"That was Lowry on the phone. He thinks you're MIA, but I told him I had talked to you. He wants us downstairs in an hour. So move it…" Rachel stopped abruptly.

"What?" I asked.

"I don't want to call you Cutter any more. Or Winston. What's your middle name?"

"Weller. It was my grandmother's maiden name."

"Well, move your ass, Weller. We need to be downstairs pronto."

We finished our breakfast and since we still had forty minutes before we had to meet Lowry, we took a very slow and very satisfying shower together. We were only twenty minutes late for our meeting. When we got to the lobby, Lowry and two other men were waiting for us. Lowry asked if we were all right and could tell by our grins we were. He didn't exactly do an eye roll, but the G-man equivalent.

"Cutter, did you get a message from Dr. Gerstner yesterday afternoon about canceling the five o'clock meeting?"

"No."

"How about on your room phone?"

"I don't know. I never checked."

"Could you run up and check now, please?" I did and there was no message, other than the three Lowry had left that morning. I reported that to him and asked why. "I had an agent meet him at his office when he arrived this morning. He told her he had canceled our meeting and seemed shocked when he learned what had happened. He claimed not to know Brandon Jones at all. He and Julie were at a dinner last night and their alibi is legit.

"He had a meeting with several of the inoculation center directors this morning, but we'll talk with him as soon as we get to the CDC office." Lowry hustled us into a waiting SUV, all black and government looking. On the way he told us Mary Beth had been moved to the hospital and was being held for observation, but seemed to be okay. "Though I think she'll need some therapy and maybe a new job, so don't count on her returning."

"What about Julie?" I asked.

"She left work sick early this morning.."

"Shouldn't you guys be talking to her? She at least would recognize Brandon's name. It was said enough around the office."

"Yeah, we want to talk to her as soon as we can find her."

We got to the CDC and a forensics van was still parked at the front door. I was shocked to see Norman Pidgeon sitting in the waiting room as we walked in. He rose to greet us and Lowry said, "Norman is going to do the audit to see if we can find the missing numbers here. He'll need you two's help he says."

Norman looked at Lowry and shook his head, then turned to us. "Can you believe this guy is military police? Unbelievable." He paused, obviously still reconciling this information with what he knew about his long-time partner. "So let's get down to their main frame room and sort this out, eh?"

"What does Marc say about all this?" Rachel asked.

Lowry answered, "Nothing, He has not been told. So if he contacts any of you, share nothing. Got it?" We all nodded. We left Lowry and headed to where their computer complex was located.

We were met there by CDC's assistant chief information officer. He was not the least bit happy having us mucking about his system. He was quick to point out Dr. Gerstner had hired Julie Barney to run a special program for the epidemiology section, and no one else was allowed to see it or work on it. In fact, contrary to normal agency policy, Gerstner and Barney were using off-site servers because Gerstner claimed the data was too sensitive for CDC servers. Turned out that information was the key for Norman to find what was being done.

Within six hours, Norman found Julie's program which randomly took numbers from our system, bypassing our recording and accounting features. Those numbers were paired with other numbers, ones which were ten digits followed by the letter M or F, then nine more digits. Those pairs were then stored in off-site servers, servers Norman was unable to access. In fact, he pronounced the firewall "brilliant" and suggested it might take a team of computer forensic specialists weeks or even months to get through it.

We briefed Lowry on Norman's discovery and Lowry asked, "So what about the incoming end. Where do the numbers originate?"

"They appear to be coming from hundreds, if not thousands, of different IP addresses."

"Can those be traced?"

Norman thought for a moment and told him, "Yeah, but it will take a while. Probably we should just run down forty or fifty to see if we get any discernible pattern."

"Can you do that from D.C.?"

"I can do that from anywhere," Norman said, almost smugly.

Lowry brought us up to date on his day. "First of all, I got the shooting cleared as a defensive shoot. I'm officially back in the field. Second, we waited for Gerstner to show up after his meeting. He didn't. I sent a team to pick up him and Julie. They're gone. In the wind. We have no idea where they are. No airline, train or bus tickets. No rental car. Their cars are still at their house. We've started the hunt, but I'd guess it will be a while before we find them."

"Now what?" I wanted to know.

"We fly back to D.C.. We're going to have someone from a different military intelligence agency question Marc. I'm too close to the situation," he paused, then added thoughtfully, "But I guess I wasn't close enough. At any rate, once again, keep your doors locked until we leave the hotel in twelve hours." It was now nine o'clock.

We returned to the hotel, I packed my bag and moved into Rachel's room for the night. Our room service dinner was cold by the time we got done ravaging each other. We didn't mind.

TWENTY-TWO

CUTTER

When we landed at Reagan National, it was one of those rare perfect spring days, the short season between the cold damp winds and high humidity swelter on the Potomac. The weather made me decide to extend our trip, not by leaving but by not going home or to the office. The entire flight back I had sat next to Rachel, holding hands and worrying. Was this new part of our relationship a reaction to the trauma we had undergone or was it just the next step? Would it hurt or help the relationship? And my job. What was going to happen there? Would AMASS continue? Was Marc involved? If AMASS went under, Rachel and I were screwed. Well, I was. She had saleable skills. Me, I got nothin'.

As we descended toward the river for our landing, I turned to Rachel and said, "It's a day for hooky. Spring fever. A picnic and bottle of wine. On a blanket in a secluded spot in the park. Oysters at a waterfront bar. Cold beer. What d'ya say?"

Lowry was in the seat in front of us and we heard him for the first time on the flight. "I'd say you got your head up your ass, Williams. Until we know what kind of threat there may be out there, you two are stuck with me or with one of my people. We picked up Marc this morning to have a little chat. He has his lawyer with him but claims he knows nothing." Lowry moved back to a seat across the aisle from us. "He says he knows Brandon, but only because they worked together for Connard Resorts. They've stayed in touch but only as acquaintances. Claims he has no knowledge of anything illegal Brandon might have been involved in. Truth is, we really have nothing but coincidence. But it's too strong of a coincidence to ignore."

Rachel asked, "So what do we do?"

"We let Norman do his work and John Harris and his folks do theirs. I think it's pretty safe to say my days at AMASS are over. I'll continue to work on the case, including making sure you guys are protected."

"Should we be scared? What about our families?"

"You should be alert. It might be an isolated issue and nothing more. We have not found a link between Brandon and Gerstner, but I suspect we will. When that happens, we might see where this leads. Hell, we don't even know why yet."

We had touched down and taxied to the gate. We followed Lowry off the plane, picked up our bags and got into yet another ominous black SUV. We went first to Rachel's condo where her daughter was waiting, along with a guy dressed in fatigues with sergeant's stripes. I shook Rachel's hand goodbye and Lowry took me to my house. Sandy, Maria and both kids were there. I frankly was a little surprised that Sandy was also there.

She spoke first. "Are you okay?" She walked over and hugged me, the kids joining in, a big ole group hug. Maria stood by the side and smiled.

"I'm fine. What happened was a shock, but it proved I'm not crazy, at least about the Cory thing."

"Michele is very interested in this. She is prepared to call for a congressional investigation if necessary."

"Let the military police and the FBI do their thing," I told her, breaking free from her embrace. I was shocked to see tears in her eyes.

"Oh, Cutter, I was so scared." Women. I'll never figure them out. Certainly not this nutty one. I spent the next couple of days with the kids and Maria. A guard stayed outside the house. Sandy also stayed, making it a little more uncomfortable, especially when I talked to Rachel, though I'm not sure why.

I did call J. Woodburn Barney to talk to him about Julie. He was a mess. I could tell over the phone. He had been notified by Lowry's team, and they had tapped his phone in case she contacted him. He wanted to know what I knew about it all. I told him what I could and tried to tell him not to worry, but that was a pretty much useless exercise. I promised to keep in touch and let him know if I heard anything.

After several days I was getting edgy. I had heard nothing from Lowry, but when I told the guard I had to go out, he did not protest and arranged for one of those SUVs to pick me up. I met Rachel for lunch. After we ate, we called Lowry and got no answer. We then tried Norman's cell phone. He didn't answer either but called us back within five minutes. He told us he was also under guard, which apparently pissed his wife off no end, and told us about his latest briefing with Lowry. They had still not located Gerstner or Julie, Marc had claimed he knew nothing, and they had yet to determine where the numbers data was going. Norman told us he was very close to finding half a dozen origins of the data and hoped to get it nailed down in the next day or two.

We were interrupted when Lowry called Rachel's cell phone. She answered and I told Norman we'd call him back. Lowry wanted Rachel to go over some of AMASS's accounts with their forensic accountants. They would be doing it at the AMASS office. She asked if I could go with her. Lowry's exact response was "if he promises not to get in the way." Sometimes I feel like tits on a boar hog. As we used to say in Iowa.

The next morning, we walked into the office together. People stared at us like we used to stare at the two-headed frog in formaldehyde in biology class. It was creepy, but you had to look. Eventually one of her clerks came over to Rachel and gave her a big hug. Then we were surrounded by folks wanting to hear all about what happened and what did it mean and was the company in trouble and what about Mary Beth and what about Julie and wasn't it something about Lowry actually being a spy. We stuck to the script Lowry had given us which told them nothing new but made them feel more a part of it. Marc was nowhere to be seen. His secretary said he was taking a few days off and wasn't to be disturbed.

Rachel went off to her office to start on the work Lowry had given her. I went into my office to twiddle my thumbs but it was soon filled with staff with lots of questions about the business. Not sure why it had not occurred to me, but the company's business had continued right along and there were actually things for me to do. Turned out it was nice to be occupied by something other than the last couple of weeks' events. KC had booked another big contract with the Department of Education, and we needed to get some staff reassigned and some new personnel in. With three of the partners gone and Marc being otherwise engaged, so to speak, KC had been running things. Quite well. She was still The Flash.

We'd been back to work a couple of weeks. Rachel had turned up nothing new or unexpected, and the investigators had left empty handed after a few days. Marc had returned to work, no worse for the wear, greeted us as he usually would, asked about how things were going and if we were alright and acknowledged how surprised he was to hear one of his partners was not what he appeared to be. It was a little eerie. On Thursday afternoon of the first week of June we got two back-to-back surprises.

First, Norman grabbed Rachel and me and took us out for coffee. He told us they had isolated two of the data generating computers and they were both from CDC's KM1 vaccination sites. He said Lowry's team was in the field going to all of the sites they could reach. Some sites were shutting down because over ninety percent of the country had been inoculated. In fact, President Connard had been on television two nights before praising himself for saving the country with his vaccination program.

Second, while we were with Norman, Lowry called to tell us Julie Barney had been found and detained. She had called her father from her room phone in the AmericInn Lodge at the outskirts of Laramie, Wyoming. She could not pay for her room, and she had not eaten for three days because her cash had run out. She told her dad she and Larry had gotten there in a friend's car which had broken down outside of town. Larry had gone out five days before to get a new car, telling her not to talk to anyone until he got back. She was scared and worried something had happened to him. When J. Woodburn asked her why she had run off, Julie told him Larry had asked her to steal tracking numbers from AMASS, and since they cost AMASS nothing and no one would notice them missing, she had done it. She was in love. Could her dad send her some money since Larry had told her she couldn't use her credit cards or cell phone? She just had to find Larry. Barney assured her she could in fact use her cards and phone.

Since her dad's phone was tapped, the police were at her door before she hung up. She had done nothing illegal so they placed her under protective custody until Lowry's unit could retrieve her. Lowry called Marc, but he refused to press charges about the theft of the numbers, and he claimed to know nothing about it. They had no grounds for arrest. Protective custody was the best they could do. At least until they had a chance to interrogate her. The FBI picked her up and flew her back to D.C..

It took less than a day for Lowry's team to find every one of the computers at the remaining inoculation sites were generating the data which was paired with an AMASS tracking number and fed into the yet undiscovered server. Lowry reported this information to John Harris who sent it up the line. Harris strongly recommended ceasing the relay of this data until it could be determined what it was and where it was going. That recommendation went all the way up the line to the Oval Office.

The president said he would have to think about it. A day later he refused to make the order.

In that day the FBI computer forensics people figured out the number, or at least part of it. The first ten digits seemed to be some unique code, the M or F indicated sex of the person being vaccinated and the last nine digits were that person's Social Security number. When that information was transmitted to CDC headquarters and Gerstner's data center, it was paired with an AMASS number and stored. Somewhere unknown. The key to understanding it finally came from the interview with Julie Barney. Lowry conducted the interview and later shared it with us.

Julie had been shocked to see one of her old bosses walk into the room. "Mr. Raleigh, what are you doing here?"

"Julie, we have a few questions we need answered before you can visit your dad, okay?"

"I guess. Has anyone heard anything from Larry yet? Has he been located?" She blushed when she said his name.

"No, we still haven't located Dr. Gerstner. We're hoping maybe something you can tell us might help us find him for you. First, could you tell us your full name and address for the record?" She did and Lowry continued, "Maybe you should start from the beginning and fill me in on what happened after you resigned from AMASS?"

A tear escaped Julie's eye and ran down her face. "Am I in trouble?"

Lowry reassured her, "We don't think so. Mr. Payton has decided not to press charges for your unauthorized use of data belonging to AMASS. So why did you subvert the system?"

"As you know, I was assigned to work on the installation of the tracking system at the Center for Disease Control. They said they were going to use the system to track the spread of disease in cases where they could tag folks who had been exposed to a disease but had not yet shown symptoms."

"Yes, I've got that."

"Larry, uh, Dr. Gerstner and I worked together on the installation and we became, uh, close." She waited for a reaction but got none so continued, "He offered me a job working for him. It would be a big increase in salary because he would hire me as a private contractor through a private funder who supported his work. I accepted and several weeks later we were talking, and he told me about this idea he was working on which might stop epidemics once and for all. Even in the case of biological warfare. The problem was he could not afford to pay for the AMASS program for what would be millions of people. He asked if there was some way I could help him do that. Maybe design a similar system or copy what AMASS did. I told him your program was protected by intellectual property law, and we could be in real trouble if I did that."

Lowry prodded her on, "So what did you do?"

"I worked out a way we could use your program and 'borrow' numbers, since there would be no cost to anyone on account of our using different servers. We decided once we proved Larry's system worked, either we could get the money to pay AMASS or maybe you would give us the numbers for the safety of our country." Julie looked at Lowry for some kind of encouragement to her thinking.

"Let's go back to those 'different servers'. Where are those servers?"

"I don't know. Larry told me he had gotten some company on the east coast to donate server space. All I was given was the IP address to use for the storage of the data."

"Okay. Tell me about the data. We know you used each person's sex and Social Security number, but what do the other ten digits do?"

"Oh, that's the ID number on the tracking device."

Lowry interrupted her, "What tracking device?"

"Larry's people had developed a very small chip which could be injected into the blood stream. When the KM1 vaccine was developed, he decided it was the perfect opportunity to implement his theory. And, Mr. Raleigh, it works! We can, I mean the CDC can track every individual in the United States." Julie seemed very pleased with herself.

Lowry ended the interview at that point and told Julie she would have to stay and answer a few more questions later. Julie asked him again to please find Dr. Gerstner. Lowry told her, "Julie, you can believe we will spare nothing to find your boyfriend."

"Oh, he's my *fiancé*," she smiled broadly.

Lowry called John Harris who called the White House directly to report. The president still refused to stop the program. Harris also ordered more agents into the field to find Larry Gerstner. The FBI, also on orders from Harris, seized samples of the vaccine over the objections of the CDC. Those samples were sent to the FBI lab in Quantico. It took just a couple of hours to discover each dose of the "vaccine" contained saline solution, sugar, a small dose of heroin, just enough to induce a mild sensation of euphoria, and hundreds of what turned out to be nano GPS chips. There was nothing to counter or prevent any disease of any kind. The president refused to stop the program, arguing mass hysteria would break out if people still believed they could contract KM1. The CDC did as it was told and continued to vaccinate, but now with just saline solution. They failed to mention that to the White House.

It took four more days to find Larry Gerstner. A man matching his description, but with entirely different identification, rented a car in Laramie the morning Julie said he disappeared. The car had a GPS unit which located it in a parking lot about a mile from the public docks in San Diego. Using both security video and agents on foot, they tracked him to where, using yet another identity, this one with a passport, he had boarded a ferry to Puerto Nuevo in Baja California, Mexico. They found him there, living in the most expensive suite at the Puerto Nuevo Baja Hotel and Villas, throwing dollars around like a rich man.

The agents ran into a snag. Because President Connard had continually disrespected Mexico and its citizens, the Mexican government refused to arrest and to extradite Gerstner. The FBI did what it always did in these situations. It called on its shadier sister, the CIA, who kidnapped the doctor, threw him on a plane and delivered him to Quantico. After he was safely locked away, Lowry released Julie to the custody of her father. He did not tell her Gerstner had been found. In fact, no one was told. He was in what they euphemistically referred to as "dark confinement". They had lots of questions for Dr. Gerstner, and the legal system and courts would not be an aid in getting answers.

Lowry briefed Rachel, Norman and me on all of this after Gerstner had been detained for about a week. We had lots of questions, of course, but led off with the only one which got answered. Rachel asked him, "Why are you telling us all this? Isn't this like classified information?"

"It is. I know all of you have security clearance at least at the lowest level. Norman's naturally has to be a little higher because of the access he has to the software used by the feds. So what I am telling you has to be kept to yourselves, at least until you read about it in the papers. Which you better never." He paused only enough for us to all nod our heads in agreement. "Considering what he was involved in, Dr. Gerstner did not hold up well to questioning. After a couple of days of interrogation, he agreed to turn state's evidence and coughed up the names of others involved in the conspiracy."

"Julie?" I asked.

He shook his head. "No, it appears she was just used. I believe she knew what she was doing was wrong, but she thought it was for all the right reasons. That she was helping our country. According to Gerstner, he and others were hired by a woman they only refer to as 'Mother' to cause a limited epidemic with germs Mother provided, then convince others in the government to vaccinate everyone with serum Mother also provided. He claims not to know anything about what was in the serum.

"He met Mother only once and described her as an attractive but older black woman, nicely dressed and with a slightly southern accent. She approached him and he agreed to do it."

"Why?" Rachel wanted to know.

"They made him very, very rich. He offered to give us the money if we would let him go." Lowry snorted a little laugh. "We had to tell him we were keeping the money and him and he would be charged with capital murder and probably sentenced to die. At that point we got an additional four names."

I was only interested in one, "Brandon?"

"Yes. But also Marc. He'll be arrested today. And AMASS will be under federal control."

TWENTY-THREE

MOTHER

Dr. Larry Gerstner reported to work at eight in the morning, expecting he would be questioned at some time during the day about the disappearance of those assholes from AMASS. He would, of course, be helpful but know nothing. He wondered if their bodies would ever show up. Instead he was greeted with the news a man had been shot in one of the labs by a federal agent who was part of the team visiting him. He was asked about missing his appointment with the team the night before. He told the detective he had called and left a message with Cutter Williams canceling the meeting. He also indicated he had no additional information to offer.

As soon as he could, he collected Julie and they walked out of the building. He drove her home, told her to pack for a trip someplace warm. When she asked him what was going on, he only said, "You have to trust me on this." He called Mother and told her Brandon had been killed and apparently one of the people from AMASS was some kind of federal agent. When Mother asked him which one, Gerstner told her, "I assume Williams, but I don't know for sure." He told Mother he was leaving and taking Julie with him.

"I should have known better than to trust someone whose only motivation is money," Mother thought to herself, but asked him if the program, so close to completion, would stop. He assured her it would not. And that there was no way they could figure out what was going on. Mother disconnected, believing Gerstner was an idiot, and he would have to be eliminated before he could do any damage to their operation. She gave not even a fleeting thought to Brandon Jones.

She thought about contacting the others involved in the program and decided against it. The last thing she needed now was for someone to panic. Besides, most did not know who was involved with them or maybe knew only one or two people. Gerstner was the only one at CDC, she had two at FEMA, but Gerstner only knew one. She had Marc at AMASS whom the doctor knew as well. Gerstner also knew one of the three at Social Security and they all knew Brandon, but that hardly mattered any more. The rest of her team was isolated from this group and no one knew about Harry Connard and Connard knew nothing of them. At most she would lose the entire operation team, all eight of them, but the operation was already a success and she could afford to do without them. Too bad, but it would save her a lot of money.

She had only two potential problems to deal with. She sent word to Connard who flew to New York to see her that night. Without telling him why, she told him no matter what he was told, he was not to allow the vaccination program to stop. She explained she had heard his political enemies were threatened by his success in this effort and would be trying to halt it before it could be finished. Mother realized the only motivation for him which was stronger than his fear of her was his need for adulation. The president assured her nothing would stop his program.

The second problem was thornier. She needed to find and neutralize Gerstner to save herself time and trouble. Problem was, with Brandon dead, she would have to use another agent which meant exposing yet another of her team to possible discovery. She decided it was worth the risk. She smiled when she remembered Gerstner had said he was taking the Barney woman with him. Gerstner was smart enough not to get himself vaccinated and tagged, but she would bet Barney had been tagged. She ran through their protocol for finding someone and was actually excited to use her system to locate someone. A win-win.

She then contacted another of her wet work agents and ordered her to eliminate their problem. She told the assassin to take her time and do it right. They could always find them when they needed to. It was one of Mother's rare mistakes.

Gerstner and Julie drove straight through from Atlanta to Laramie, Wyoming, almost twenty-four hours. Their SUV, which had been stolen and hidden months before for just such a use, blew a head gasket. Larry decided they needed to stop anyway, gather their thoughts and determine the best way to get out of the country. Over dinner at a cowboy bar downtown he told Julie they needed to decide where they wanted to go. Julie was still worried about why they were running, but she trusted him. She said offhandedly, "Well, at least we don't have to worry about KM1 if they have it wherever we go."

Gerstner did his best not to choke on his bison burger. Fuck, he'd forgotten about her GPS chip. He hurried her through dinner and back to the hotel. He told her he wanted to get to sleep so he could get up early to find someone to fix their car. He made love to her one last time. At six in the morning he left without waking her, made his way to a rental agency, got a car and two days later was at the docks in San Diego. The following day he sat on the beach, drinking *cerveza* and ogling young bodies, feeling smart and lucky. He had lots of money and his freedom. Life was good.

Eight days later he was still drunk and shacked up with an American college girl in a fancy suite, the best money could buy. He sent the girl out to get them another bottle of tequila and within minutes of her leaving, there was a knock on the door. When he answered, two men shoved him back into the room, gave him a shot and the next thing he knew, he was in a cell somewhere.

Mother's killer-for-hire watched from her car as two men dragged her target from his room and loaded him into a truck. She had to tell Mother, and she knew Mother was not going to be happy. But then Mother had told her not to hurry. When the doctor deserted the Barney woman in Wyoming, it took a while to find him. A day too late.

Mother was not upset with her agent, she was upset with herself. Still she knew her losses would be well worth the gain. She flew to Paris to meet with the president of her country. He was pleased with the progress, even though her agents had been blown. In fact, he couldn't have cared less if they died. He assured her they had already gained more than they needed to achieve their goals.

"What do you mean, sir?" Mother asked him.

"Our analysts have been doing research and projections on how our President Connard's policies will affect the country over the next twenty years. It appears his divisiveness, his stripping of social programs and his continuing to do everything within his power to make the rich richer will take the country to a breaking point."

"How?"

The president of Russia smiled. "It will be just like in our country in 1917. The very few will have too much and the very many will have too little. There will be open rebellion." He smiled even more broadly, "And your program, your brilliant program, will allow us to support those who would be our friends in their efforts to overthrow the country and bring it under our control. We will not lose a single Russian life as America destroys itself."

TWENTY-FOUR

CUTTER

The FBI showed up at AMASS that morning, read Marc his rights and placed him under arrest. He glared at everyone as he was led, handcuffed, out the door. Lowry called everyone together for a staff meeting.

"Good morning all," he started. The room was filled with somber and questioning faces. He went on, "I'm sure what just happened is a shock to most of you, and I can't really discuss the case, but it probably does not involve AMASS and it definitely does not involve any of you. Since you are all aware of my position…"

He was interrupted by a programmer named Pankaj from the back of the room, "I do not know. Would you please to explain?"

Lowry went on, "I'm sorry. As most of you already know, while I was working here, my real job was with the military. I was responsible for insuring the military's proper use of manpower. At any rate, I am no longer affiliated with AMASS and my share of the company ownership actually belongs to the U.S. government. Because of his arrest, Marc's controlling share also falls under the control of the government." There were numerous groans from the group. "But as far as you are concerned, your positions will not change. Many agencies still need your services, and it is our hope you will continue to provide those services. Finally, the two remaining partners, Norman and Rachel, will assume leadership with Rachel acting as CEO."

Again from Pankaj, "Should not Mr. Pidgeon be the big boss?"

Now Norman spoke up, "No thank you. I really have no desire to be CEO. Ms. Red Cloud will do a fine job, and I want all of you to help her in any way you can." There were a few more murmurings and questions, but within the hour everyone was back at work and smiling. Truth be told, almost everyone had at one point or another had an ass chewing from Marc and everyone was a little afraid of him. No one was afraid of Rachel. Except maybe me.

Just like that our lives slipped back into normalcy, or what I had come to see as normalcy. I fixed breakfast for the kids, Sandy was gone from Monday morning to Friday evening, and Jordan and Livingston spent most of their time wrapped up in their friends' lives. Livingston was turning eight and Jordan was fourteen, that age where her parents were idiots and her mom was the mortal enemy. I'm pretty sure Jordan understood what was going on with us and with her mom in particular, but she never said anything about it. When her friends brought up Sandy's continual absence, Jordan played the "my mom is very important" card.

Rachel and I seemed to be caught in limbo. We occasionally spent the night together at her townhouse and she came over for dinner and the evening a couple of times a week. I still was in love with her, but we still never talked about it. She was, as I always thought she would be, a great boss. AMASS continued to thrive.

We heard nothing about Marc, the KM1 inoculation program (until the president called a press conference to announce it as his latest great achievement), nor about who was behind the plot.

In late September I got a call from Congresswoman Buday's office asking me to come in and meet with her. Her secretary suggested eight the next morning. I agreed.

"Thank you so much for coming in on such short notice," Michele said to me. "I think it only fair, since you are the one who more or less started this whole thing, to bring you up to date. Understand this is all classified information and falls under the laws which protect that type of information. Do you agree?" I told her I did, though I knew at some point it would drive me crazy and I would have to share it with Rachel. She went on, "That means even with your wife. Sandy knows some of this, but not all. Understand?" I nodded.

"We have in custody seven people, including Marc Payton and Larry Gerstner. All except Marc worked for the government. We have made no headway into discovering what country or organization is behind this program. All of them have admitted their parts in the plot, but only that they work for someone they call 'Mother'. We have yet to locate her."

"We asked each one how they were recruited. Most were approached directly by Mother and only met her once. Until he died, Brandon Jones was their contact. Marc's story for meeting her did not hold up under close scrutiny. After more intense questioning" and here Michele raised her eyebrows, "we learned something kind of shocking about Marc Payton." Now I raised my eyebrows. "He isn't Marc Payton. He is Anthony Payton, Marc's twin brother."

I made an involuntary sound which sounded a lot like a gasp. "You're kidding me," I said though I realized the congresswoman probably didn't do a lot of kidding. "What does that mean?"

"It means this program has been in the planning a long, long time. It also means two of the conspirators, Anthony and Brandon, worked for Harry Connard before he became president. That is most troubling." Though she smiled when she said it.

"Do you know why Cory Jones died? Did this Anthony order him killed?"

"We think so, but we don't know for sure. We do know Brandon Jones was in Spain at the same time. Maybe Cory had actually found something, though it is more probable Anthony just didn't want him snooping around. These are not nice people. Killing tens of thousands meant nothing to them."

"So what happens now?"

"Several things. First, I am going to call for a hearing under the rules for classified military intelligence, which means all in *sub rosa*."

"Will I have to testify? Or any of the other people there when Brandon was shot?"

"Only Major Raleigh. You will be referred to," and here she stopped to smile, "as a 'confidential informant'. We need to determine if there are others involved, where the GPS identification information has gone, how it might be used and how far up the chain here this goes." I was sure she was referring to the president.

"You said there were several things. What else?"

"Our technicians have discovered a means to neutralize the GPS nano chips in everyone's body. If a person is exposed to an electromagnetic-wave bombardment for as little as three seconds, the chips are disabled. Problem is, first the machines which can do that will have to be built, then we'll have to figure out how to get everyone through one without telling them why. We believe if the general public ever finds out about what really has happened, there would be mass hysteria. Not good."

"So how can that be done?"

"What our folks think is we do it surreptitiously over a long period of time, unless we become aware of some serious imminent threat from the information being out there. By incorporating it into security scanners, medical scanners and the like. Pretty much everyone goes through one at some time or another. In the end, the only thing whoever has this information will have is everyone's Social Security number. Admittedly, that's not a good thing, but we can live with that. Banks and medical organizations already have the information anyway. There was some talk about our using the technology for our own uses, but wiser heads prevailed." She paused, then added, "Of course, we did not share that with the president."

"What about the KM1 virus? Is it still a threat?"

"We don't think so. Apparently the perpetrators infected those patient zero people and did it in isolated areas to control the outbreak. But because of that, everyone involved will face the death penalty. Unless, of course, they agree to plead guilty and to testify at our committee hearings. If so, they will be sentenced to life in prison. And they will be in solitary confinement at least until we have totally eliminated any threat from these GPS trackers."

I sat, shaking my head. "Anything else?"

"I don't think so, Cutter. You should know your government is very appreciative of your help. But it can't go any further. There won't be any parades in your honor." She smiled, but I could tell she was dead serious. She turned thoughtful and added, "Pretty amazing when you think about it. Other than providing the germs and the serum, whoever did this did it on the U.S. taxpayers' tab. Hundreds of millions spent and more millions to be spent. If it wasn't so bad for us, I would call it brilliant." Her voice trailed off.

"Thank you for sharing all this with me, Congresswoman," I told her.

"I thought you deserved to be told. I doubt we will speak of this again, but I do hope to cross paths with you in the future. And do call me if I can do anything for you at any time." She rose and I knew that was the cue for me to leave. She shook my hand and said, "Sandy would like to speak with you before you leave, if you have a few minutes."

By the time I said "Certainly. And thank you," she had guided me to the door. I took a seat in the waiting room and ten minutes later an aide showed me to Sandy's office.

As I entered, Sandy came forward and gave me a big hug. She held me for a full minute, head buried in my chest. I wasn't quite sure what to make of it, but I hugged her back. She released me, eyes on the ground, walked over and closed the door. She went to her couch, sat down and patted the seat next to her. The last time she had done that was years ago in our Iowa office and then she was inviting me to get laid. I was pretty sure that's not what she was doing now. I sat.

"Winston, Stephen and I bought a house in Des Moines and are moving back there." I'm not sure what she saw on my face, but my first, my only thought was "Not with my kids, you're not." She put her hands up in a defensive matter as if my look had conveyed I wanted to slug her. Which I did, I guess. In fact, she had read my mind. She quickly added, "I don't want to move the kids. I want them to stay here with you, if that's alright." I relaxed.

"Tell me," I said.

"The congresswoman is going to run for Senate next year. She believes the time has come to unseat that pompous male Republican asshole from the dark ages. And she wants me to run for her seat. With her endorsement. She's sure we both can win." Her speech was in hyper drive, as if she were afraid if I interrupted or she didn't get it all out, we would get into a big fight. She was probably right. I could barely follow her, let alone respond.

"So I need to be a resident of Iowa again. And obviously the voters there will not accept our, what, 'arrangement' considering how conservative they are. So we need to get a dissolution and I need to marry Stephen. I have the papers all drawn up and all you have to do is sign them. We share custody, you get the house, you get Maria, I pay for half of all the kids' expenses and we split our holdings 50-50." She finally slowed to take a breath.

"Does Stephen have any idea what he's getting himself into?" She shot me that look which used to sear into my soul and make me feel small and worthless. Now it only entertained me because I knew I had hit a nerve. Which made me realize she was exactly right. It was time to part ways.

"Okay. Where are the papers?" I asked.

She stared at me, not responding for a long time. We just looked into each other's eyes and knew. She went to her desk, picked up a folder and a pen and brought them to me. She left me to read and sign and went out of her office. About ten minutes later when I was done, she walked back into the room and handed me one of two matching cut crystal glasses. She raised hers and we clinked. An airplane gin and tonic. I have to admit, it showed a lot of style. It was, in a word, perfect. We drank our drinks and I rose to leave.

"Cutter, if it's alright with you, I would like to take the children to Iowa for Thanksgiving week. That's when we'll make the announcement about my candidacy. Please?"

I walked over to her, hugged her like I meant it, because I did, and told her that would be fine, but I wanted the kids for Christmas. She smiled and nodded and I left without another word being said.

You know, I would really like to be able to tell you how it all felt. I'm not sure I can. I was hollow and happy all at the same time. Sad and expectant. Relieved and scared. I remember sitting on the Metro and smiling with tears rolling down my cheeks. I was on the yellow line and rode all the way to Huntington Station, the end of the line. Then rode it all the way back to the other end at Mt. Vernon, got off and walked around the city until I had just enough time to get back to my car and get home to pick up the kids for dinner. I was never so happy to see them.

Friday evening, Sandy came for dinner, bringing with her the dissolution decree. The congresswoman had a judge friend who had expedited the process. Of course she did. We were officially single again. At least I wasn't a two-time loser like she was.

We explained to the kids what was going to happen. Sandy couched it all in how important it was to the country that she get elected and how this would be the kids' chance to help that effort. Christ in a hand basket, divorce as a patriotic act. The kids acted pretty much as I figured they would. Jordan got pissed and refused to talk, Livingston bottled it up and refused to talk. Sandy counted silence as a win. I knew I would deal with the fallout later, after Sandy retreated. I did. It was not pleasant. Jordan did seem to find solace in two things. One, I seemed okay with it and, two, she would fit right in with her two best friends who proudly proclaimed at every opportunity, "I'm from a broken home."

I had told Rachel all about the report I received from the congresswoman. I told her nothing about the report from Sandy. I'm not sure why. Maybe I wanted to digest it all myself before it could get tangled up with my feelings for Rachel. Maybe I wanted to make sure I was going to be okay and not too damaged to get involved, though it could hardly be called a rebound romance. Finally, I said, "Fuck it," and asked Rachel if she wanted to go down to a bed and breakfast in Annapolis for the weekend. When she started to ask what was up, I put my finger to her lips and told her we needed to talk at length, but I thought it would be a good thing. She agreed.

I could tell you all about our weekend, but suffice it to say, it went well, she was happy and the rest would just appeal to your prurient interests. On our drive back Sunday, we took the long way around and caught the first of the leaves changing, It was one of those crisp early fall days and it fit the mood perfectly. We had driven up to an overlook and parked, sitting in silence. Finally, I said, "Rachel, you are probably the best friend I have ever had. I'm not sure how I can ever thank you for all you have done for me." She smiled. I added, "And to me." She hit me in the shoulder and grinned.

"You could take me to Paris. I've always wanted to go."

"How about Thanksgiving week?" She smiled and nodded her head.

In early November Lowry Raleigh came to take me to lunch. He rehashed most of what the congresswoman had told me, though since she had sworn me to secrecy, I couldn't tell him that. He did add two things. Someone had gotten to Dr. Larry Gerstner in prison and stabbed him thirty-one times. It happened two days after Gerstner decided not to plead guilty and to stand trial. Lowry said he didn't believe the government was involved. But he wasn't sure. The other thing was the president had been subpoenaed and was to testify the Monday after Thanksgiving.

We slid through the next few weeks and the kids seemed to grow more comfortable with the new arrangement, especially since they got to go spend weekends at their mom's. Jordan predictably hated Stephen, but Livingston pronounced him, "Okay." When they returned on Sunday evening, Maria would yell at them, in Spanish, for eating too many sweets and then hug them as if she had not seen them for months. The closer we got to Thanksgiving the more excited they became. They were going to get to see their

Surface grandparents and be on stage for their Mom's announcement. She had bought them new outfits to wear for the occasion. No doubt picked out for political expediency.

The Friday before Thanksgiving, Rachel Red Cloud and I flew to Paris, Air France, first-class. Courtesy of a joint account Sandy did not know she and I had. I felt not one bit guilty. We stayed at the *Hôtel des Grandes Écoles*, two blocks from the Pantheon, and spent our days doing everything Paris: the Louvre, Notre Dame, tiny restaurants, the Seine, Montmartre, croissants, the Eiffel Tower, the Champs-Élyséées stores. On Thanksgiving Day, it was rainy and we spent the afternoon at Shakespeare and Company, more for the ambience than the books. We ended up in an inexpensive little Greek restaurant in the Latin Quarter for dinner, the Acropolis on *Rue Xavier Privas*. The food was mediocre, if I'm being generous.

We ordered a couple of glasses of cheap wine and some food. The wine came quickly, the food did not. We talked about what a great week it had been and how much we loved Paris and how we would have to come back many more times. During a lull in the conversation, Rachel asked me, "Weller, if Sandy had decided to come back, what would have happened to us?"

I just looked at her. My mind said "I have no fucking idea," but my mouth fortunately remained mute. I really could not answer her question. It actually scared me a little to think about it. "Well?"

The famous Cutter wit and charm leapt into action. "Rachel, do you want to get married?" Before she could answer, I clarified, "To me?"

She had been frowning. It took a minute but the frown left and was replaced with a very serious look. "Yes. Yes, I do." And she cried. The famous Cutter wit and charm could not help me. I cried as well.

We ate what was the worst meal we ever had in Paris and talked about our future. It was the first time it had ever happened and it was exciting. Instead of going straight back to the hotel, we walked over to Notre Dame and went inside, where Rachel knelt and prayed. I was afraid to ask what that was all about, so I never did.

When we returned to the hotel, our hostess came to our room and told us we should come to the lobby to see the television. We followed her back and learned President Harry Connard had been found dead in the penthouse of his Manhattan hotel, apparently from a heart attack. He was alone when he died, according to the reports. Mike Shilling had been sworn in as the new president.

EPILOGUE

I'm sitting in my childhood bedroom on a now rarely used bed. I used to share this room with my brothers Jim and John. They were older, but I never got to have a room to myself because John never left home. When Jim left, I got to move to a top bunk, but that was as close to having my own room as I ever got. It's Christmastime in Iowa, snow on the ground and butt freezing cold outside. Rachel is in the bottom bunk across the room still sleeping. I love to watch her face when she sleeps. It has a softness that makes me feel completely at peace. The kids are staying at their Aunt Patti's with their cousins who are teenagers like Jordan. Livingston wanted to stay with "the big kids".

I've been reading over this account which J. Woodburn Barney and I put together over the last few months about the things that happened to all of us. It's been over a year since all this happened but still feels like yesterday. It was especially tough on old man Barney because of what his daughter went through. Julie never did find out the truth of what her lover Larry Gerstner had done to the citizens of his country. In fact, Julie does not know what happened to the doctor. As far as she is concerned, he left her and has never resurfaced. I kind of hope she never learns about his dying in prison. Julie now lives in Holland, Michigan and works at a bookstore. I understand from her dad she just started dating a professor at Hope College and that she is finally getting over her depression. Good for her.

This account can never be made public, of course, without me facing prosecution for revealing classified information, but Barney agreed we should write it down so the story was recorded somewhere. Obviously, a lot of what J. Woodburn has written is pure conjecture—remember what I told you about writers making things up? Funny thing though, when I presented these theories to Lowry Raleigh, he did not deny any of them. And Congresswoman Buday? She smiled that little crooked tooth smile of hers and said, "The only thing I can tell you, Cutter, is, had Harry Connard survived, he would have been impeached. And most likely, convicted."

Lowry was pretty good about letting me know where things stood. If there is a hero in this story, it's Lowry. He's now a colonel and, best as I can tell, he is now one of those John Harris people, giving orders and running spy rings. Or some such nonsense. He and I have lunch from time to time. He catches me up on the latest and because he still can't remember his wallet, I buy the lunches. I don't mind. He saved my life.

One thing Lowry told me was the classified information about Harry Connard's death. Apparently Connard had a longtime girlfriend he kept squirreled away in the penthouse of his New York City hotel. According to the Secret Service, he visited her on a pretty regular basis. He went to visit her the night before Thanksgiving, as he had done in the past. He normally just spent a couple of hours with the woman, so after six hours, the agents broke in and found him dead. There was no trace of the woman.

It took several more hours for them to find a hidden elevator which went straight to the parking garage underground. The woman had vanished and the information they had on her turned out to be false. She was not who they thought she was. When he told me this, Lowry was smiling and he added, "Had it been any other president and had the intelligence community not known what they knew, the Secret Service would have been in a lot of trouble." He went on to explain the surgeon general herself had done the autopsy and had found a small puncture wound in Connard's arm which she omitted from the autopsy report. I asked what that meant.

"It opens up the possibility Connard's heart attack was brought on by air being injected into his bloodstream. Impossible to trace, almost always fatal if the air bubble is large enough." He went on to tell me the hunt continued for a black woman who was called "Mother" by her agents and who, according to descriptions, might very well have been Connard's lover. Or handler. Or both.

The last time we had lunch about a month ago, I asked about the technology to neutralize the GPS units. He asked "You flown anywhere lately?" I shook my head. He added, "Next time you fly and go through security, your little bugs will be killed. No one will be able to track you again." When we flew out here to Iowa, we all took the cure, so to speak.

Shortly after the first of the year, the folks at AMASS and his remaining family held a memorial service for Marc. We attended and it was sad. Marc, the real Marc, sounded like he must have been a hell of a guy. His wife, his widow, collected a huge life insurance policy that the real Marc had held. She seemed quite at peace. Even Lowry was there. No one mentioned Anthony.

Rachel and I are no longer with AMASS. After Anthony/Marc pled guilty and was sentenced to prison with no chance of parole, AMASS became the property of the United States government. Norman and Rachel were given buyouts for their fifteen percent shares. It was a lot of money. There is no doubt in my mind the government was very generous in their evaluation of the worth of the company because of Norman and Rachel's contributions to uncovering what had happened. Norman retired. Rachel had enough money to retire. I quit because I just could not stand the idea of working for a government entity again. I'm still keeping my options open. Which means I haven't found a job yet. Not that I have been seriously looking, though one of these days I suppose I'll have to.

After AMASS became a government agency, Karen "The Fulton Flash" Miller was named director. She now prefers to be called Director Miller. I'll always call her The Flash. The government couldn't have made a better choice. Most everyone else stayed with the organization which is now known as the Office of Personnel Strategies. Somehow it seems fitting The Flash is Director of OOPS. Government acronyms. How can you not love them? Mary Beth Irelan finally returned from her long leave of absence. The Flash told me she is doing quite well and is her old bubbly self.

Within days after our dissolution, Sandy married Stephen Scott. Her announcement of her candidacy for congress was to follow Michele Buday's announcement for the senate race. Both were delayed by the unexpected passing of Harry Connard, but both candidates declared before year's end. As promised, Jordan and

Livingston got to wear their new outfits and stand on stage with their mommy and new daddy. They looked like the perfect Iowa family, a candidate right out of a Norman Rockwell painting.

It turned out both candidates were given a huge advantage in their campaigns. If most of America had decided electing Connard was a big mistake, within three months of his ascendency to the presidency, most voters had developed a real hatred for Mike Shilling. He was exactly what he had seemed to be. A bigot, homophobe, misogynist and intellectual weakling. His first act as president was to introduce legislation to have Christianity named as the official religion of the country and to bar all other religions. He then introduced legislation outlawing homosexuality, followed by legislation to strip nonwhites and women of their voting rights. While these may have been the aims, in one form or another, of many Republicans, they had to disclaim such a blatant approach to the dismantling of American principles. None of his legislation made it out of committee and Republican officials ran for the hills. They refused to nominate him for another term as president.

With the Republican party in disarray and with the general electorate fed up with D.C. shenanigans and the spiraling inflation that had followed ill-advised Republican economic policies, the Democrats swept control of both houses of congress and the presidency. James Breiner finally got his shot at running the country. To help him were the newly elected Senator Michele Buday and newly elected Congresswoman Sandra Scott. I'll never look at that name and title without smiling. I think Sandy finally got what she wanted. Power, prestige and her father's respect. I am happy for her. Especially from a distance. She and her husband live in a townhouse twenty minutes away from the kids who still live with me.

Jordan and Livingston? Doing fine as near as I can tell. They've adjusted to having two families, Jordan has decided she has to talk to her mother now that she's famous, and Livingston, well, he's decided he's going to be an astronaut and tells everyone his mom can get him the job.

Rachel and I were married on the beach outside Hatteras Village at the Outer Banks. I wore seersucker shorts and no shoes. Rachel wore a clingy white almost see-through beach dress and no shoes. Jordan and Elena were co-maids of honor. Livingston was best man. Most of my family was there. Patti did all the planning and my mom did all the bossing. Rachel's mother and brothers flew in from the Four Corners. The family was more interested in their new Native American in-laws than they were in the bride and groom. Mom made a new best friend within ten minutes of meeting Rachel's mom. Friends from D.C. came down and even the mayor of Columbus, Colorado, Ham and Eggs, and his wife joined us. Aside from the day Livingston was born, it was the best day of my life.

I am still very worried about this country. The last five years have torn us down to the very roots. We are a splintered society and there is a lot of unhappiness and unrest. I hope, for our sakes and the sakes of our children, we can fix it. Hate is a hard thing to break, almost impossible to banish. It will take the new congress and president years just to rectify the damage done recently. And for me there is always the specter of some outside entity, maybe the Russians, maybe someone else, which wants to destroy our way of life. Yet, you gotta get up in the morning and do what you can do to make things better. More voters turned out this last election, but there is still way too much apathy. Maybe I should look for work somewhere I might be able to make a difference.

It's Christmas Eve morning and I've heard voices downstairs, most likely Mom and John. John and his wife Becky are the only other family here right now and no way is Becky up before nine. Mom probably has a big pot of coffee on and I can smell her homemade cinnamon rolls baking. Even though she is in her eighties, she has most likely already been outside in her quilted robe and her knee high rubber boots to sneak a cigarette. We all pretend not to notice her vice.

I just looked up from typing this addendum to our story and Rachel is up on one elbow, watching me. "What?" I ask her.

"Tell me something, would you?" she says, her voice low and serious.

"If I can."

"How did you get the name Cutter?"

I smile and rise and walk over to her bunk bed. Instead of telling her, I decide to find out if she still likes mornings best.

ACKNOWLEDGEMENTS

When people I know ask about my writing, they almost always want to know, not about the story I'm working on, but about the writing process. With this book, when they asked, my answer was "it goes in fits and starts". Shaped more by the world around me than the world in me, this work was slow in developing. I would write some and get distracted, sometimes weeks on end. What brought me back to the story most frequently were those folks who had a line or a thought or a musing they believed should be in a book and they wanted to share it with me. Like Peter Bugg, who called one night from Phoenix to share his "Jimmy Buffett title, beach novels and airport bars". Sometimes they made it into the book, sometimes not. But the encouragement always sent me back to the story. So a general thanks to anyone who asked.

If one is lucky, and I am, one gets to meet interesting people with interesting stories as they wander through life. The genesis of this book was a story one of the best bosses I ever had, Mark Newsome, told about his days in military intelligence. He and his partners and some of the folks at their firm served as jumping off places for characters in the book. A special shout out to Mark, James Tillman (manpower guru), Walter Lilius (software guru), Casey Feller (the real Fulton Flash), Barb Belville (who kept everything together) and Pankaj Lawande (asker of great questions). The characters in the book share only the good traits with these folks. Thanks for the inspiration.

Two brothers, Brandon and Cory Jones, wanted to be in a book like their father, the infamous Ken "Black Bart" Jones, had been. Guys, be careful what you wish for, cause sometimes you get it. A special thanks to Cory who actually did run with the bulls in Pamplona and sent me back the description of his adventure. He is quoted word for word in the email which stuck in Cutter's craw. Great writing, Cory! Brandon posed as Cutter for the cover. It was the first time he had been in a suit in a decade, so a special thanks to him.

The people who turn the manuscript into a book have become a well-oiled team and I've learned to stay out of their way while they do a fantastic job. Deborah, my wife, muse, critic and editor. Samantha Varner down at AppalachianAcorn Publishing, who also offers comments and does the blurbs. Patti Hicks, who reads the story as I go along to make sure things keep moving in the direction they should. And who is the inspiration for Cutter's sister Patti.

Nathan Lewis took Brandon's photograph, worked some magic and put Cutter in front of the Kremlin. Tad Barney again created a cover to make us all look good. And Jerry Picker, just because.

For this book, the following friends and family loaned their names to my characters: Sandy Surface, Karen and Charlie Miller, Ted Rundio, Michele Buday, Julie Barney, Ellen Thordason, Peter Bugg, William Hoy, Kathy Frye, Larry Gerstner, Mary Beth Irelan, James Breiner, Dr. David Gilmore, John Harris, Whitney Husz, Elena de Alvare and Weller Callaham.

To my readers, Thanks!!!!!

Contact the author at jameswbarney@gmail.com

What readers have to say about *Cutter* and *Cutter Director's Cut*

Cutter

"Mr. Barney's writing is descriptive and witty."

"Excellent book, well written and hard to put down! Very interesting look at behind the scenes politics."

"Cutter is a great debut novel."

"...a fast, magnetic read"

"...a highly satisfying tale"

"A very well written and well thought out story"

"I loved the writing style."

"Barney is a natural storyteller with a talent for character development."

Cutter Director's Cut

"Great sequel. Cutter is a tremendously human character."

"This is a remarkable book by a very talented writer."

"Characters were well defined and captured my interest. A very good read."

"Barney's second novel captures the hilarious and sleazy side of politics and the public sphere."

"Excellent story and character development."

"Cutter is a character with heart."

"Wicked wit."

Kirkus Reviews says of **Cutter Director's Cut**

"A twisty tale of an ordinary man overcoming treachery."

Made in the USA
Monee, IL
20 September 2022